John Bigelow

Emanuel Swedenborg

Servus domini

John Bigelow

Emanuel Swedenborg
Servus domini

ISBN/EAN: 9783337723057

Printed in Europe, USA, Canada, Australia, Japan

Cover: Foto ©Raphael Reischuk / pixelio.de

More available books at **www.hansebooks.com**

EMANUEL SWEDENBORG

SERVUS DOMINI

BY

JOHN BIGELOW

———

NEW YORK & LONDON

G. P. PUTNAM'S SONS

1888

EMANUEL SWEDENBORG,

SERVUS DOMINI.

———————

AMONG the men who have been instrumental in con-
tributing to the moral and spiritual progress of our kind,
there is no one in any age who has claimed to have rendered a more important service than Emanuel Swedenborg. If we can accept his own declarations, he was the
immediate instrument of the Lord in making intelligible
to men a new and incalculably important order of truths,
upon a class of subjects which most directly affect man's
spiritual nature and destiny; he claimed to have explored
entirely new and unattempted regions of truth, to have
discovered new degrees of human faculties, their qualities, their laws of action and development; to have
entered consciously into the highest realms of spiritual
existence, and to have brought away with him a full, clear
and absolutely authentic account of what he observed of
the new and better worlds to which he was admitted.

His reports were listened to at first with distrust or
derision. They gradually arrested the attention of a few
thoughtful men who took the trouble to study and explain them. His hierophants rapidly assumed the propor-
tions of a sect. And it is not to be denied that the steadily
increasing influence which his teachings are exerting upon
human society is a phenomenon in some respects quite
unprecedented. The American Swedenborg Printing and
Publishing Society was organized and has been sustained
for a quarter of a century, exclusively for the publishing
and popularizing of his writings. This Society, with other
agencies in the United States, has supplied not less than
fifteen hundred libraries with his works, and has circulated

about sixty thousand copies of them besides. Through the liberality of Mr. Iungerich, a zealous disciple of Swedenborg, 26,703 copies of the *True Christian Religion*, and 19,690 copies of the *Apocalypse Revealed*, both large and costly works, have been furnished gratuitously to all the clergy, of whatever religious denomination, that have expressed a desire to possess them. The American New Church Tract and Publication Society has supplied the clergy gratuitously with 24,944 copies of his work on *Heaven and Hell.* The same Society also distributes annually over two hundred thousand tracts and kindred publications, designed to present the doctrines of the "New Church" in a popular form. The British and Foreign Swedenborg Society, established in 1810, have distributed by way of donation among colleges, public institutions, the clergy and others, between seven and eight thousand volumes of his writings, in addition to their annual sales, ranging for many years past from five to seven thousand volumes. The annual sales of the tracts of the English tract societies range between forty and fifty thousand a year.

In other countries the demand for "New Church" literature has also been more or less remarkable. Some or all of Swedenborg's works have been published in the Latin, Sanscrit-Hindu, French, Swedish, German, Icelandic, Italian, Norwegian, Russian, Spanish, Dutch, Polish, and Welsh languages, and every year is adding to the number made accessible by translation to new classes of readers in every quarter of the globe.

It is an axiom in history that "a religion that does not propagate itself and its sacred books is either dying or dead." If the converse of this be true, that the religion that does propagate itself and its sacred books is alive and flourishing, there is no branch of the Christian Church that exhibits more vitality than that with which the name of Swedenborg has been associated.

It is more than a century since this illustrious Swede commenced the publication of his theological writings. They were all written in the Latin tongue; were published at his own expense, in very limited editions, and the earlier ones without his name. Most of the copies were presented by him to public libraries, or to personal friends supposed to be interested in the subjects of them. No special effort was made in his life-time to attract public attention to their contents. The press of the period seems scarcely to have known of their existence. Quietly, but steadily, however, they have gained readers, and their doctrines, converts, until now his disciples may be found in every Christian land; his works in the language of every civilized people; and his doctrines more or less leavening the pulpit teachings of every Christian sect. This growth and vitality of a comparatively modern system of religious instruction and Biblical interpretation is in many respects without a precedent. It would, I think, be difficult to name an instance of any other society organized expressly for the propagation and exposition of the teachings of an uninspired writer that has been maintained for any considerable fraction of such a period of time as has elapsed since the writings of Swedenborg were first submitted to the public. Of all the founders of schools of thought since the Apostles, I recall none to whom such homage has been paid.

This vitality seems to be the more exceptional and extraordinary from the fact that Swedenborg took no steps looking to the foundation of a sect. He not only disclaimed in the most explicit terms any such purpose, but he lived and died a communicant of the Lutheran Church, in which he was reared. To whatever conclusion, therefore, one may come in regard to his authority as a teacher of theology, it is clear that he belonged to an order of men very rare in the world, who brought extraordinary gifts to the study of the most important problems of human life; and that the wisest may learn much from his writings, while no one can afford to make light of his extraordinary influence, nor of the means by which he acquired it.

I.

1688–1710.

EMANUEL SWEDENBORG was born at Stockholm, in Sweden, on the 29th day of January, 1688, and died on the 29th day of March, 1772, having attained the then unusual age of eighty-four years.   His life divides itself into three sharply-defined periods.

First, the period of his childhood and Academic life, reaching to 1710.

Second, the Scientific period, from 1710 to 1742.

Third, the "Illuminated" period, from 1742 to 1772.

Swedenborg was descended from a family of successful and opulent miners. He was the third child of Jesper Swedberg, who attained successively the positions of chaplain of the Court in 1688 ; Pastor of Wingaker in 1690 ; professor in the University of Upsala in 1692 ; Dean of the cathedral in Upsala in 1694 ; superintendent of the Swedish churches in America, London, and Portugal in 1696 ; and Bishop of Skara in 1703. The father was chaplain at Court when Emanuel was born, and by his fearless, straight-forward and truly apostolic demeanor, soon won the entire confidence of his King. He commenced his duties as chaplain by exercising his regiment, consisting of 1,200 men, in the catechism. In a voluminous Autobiography which he left behind him in MS., he tells us :—"To this they were quite unused, so that when they saw me coming they quailed more than they ever did before the enemy. But when I began telling them stories from the Bible in a quiet way, they soon came to like me so well that they did not care to go away when their time was up and another detachment was to come in, so that between the two I was near being trampled under their feet. The officers, too, sat at the table listening and exchanging with me edifying remarks. At one yearly muster of the regiment I told them that the next year I should give a catechism to each man who should be able to read it, at the same time taking down the names of those who could then read, numbering three hundred. The next year I found six hundred who could read, and it cost me six hundred copper dollars to redeem my promise. I betook myself to the King, told him of the expense I had incurred, and he at once pulled out his purse filled with ducats, and gave me a handful without counting them."

Father Swedberg was no time-server, and neither found nor sought one way for the rich and powerful and another

for the poor and feeble, to get to heaven. He was a strict
disciplinarian ; he insisted upon the observance of the Sab-
bath, and exhibited a blunt and honest persistency in the
discharge of his duties, which, though irksome to those
to whom all religious restraints are irksome, and involving
him in no end of trouble, pleased the King very much.
One day his Majesty said to him, "You have many en-
.emies." " True," said the chaplain, " the servant of the
Lord, your Majesty, is not good for much who has not
enemies." On another occasion, the King, under an im-
pulse of gratitude for something he had done, said, "Ask
what you like, and you shall have it."

" From that day," Swedberg tells us, "I became more
earnest and wary in all I said or did. I asked nothing
for myself nor mine, no, not the half of a stiver ; but
spoke to the king freely of meritorious poor men, and he
always attended to my suggestions. I also pleaded for
schools, colleges, and for the diffusion of religious publications. When he asked me who should be appointed to
a vacant living, I named the person I thought best fitted
for it, and he always got it. Hence many good men came
into rich livings, to their joyful surprise, and without any
suspicion of the cause. As I found every day freer access
to his Majesty, I prayed with my whole heart unto God
that I might not become proud nor misuse my opportunities, but that he would consecrate me to His service and
glory ; and that I might fulfil my every duty with watch-
fulness, never forgetting that Court favor is capricious, and
that I was surrounded with gossips and backbiters. Moreover I laid down these two rules for myself: first, to med-
dle in no affairs, political or worldly, with which I had no
business. And second, never to speak ill of any one,
should he even be my worst enemy and persecutor."

His Episcopate over the Swedish church in Pennsyl-
vania furnished the bishop with the occasion for publishing
a little work, made up of reports from his clergy there,
entitled *America Illuminata, written and published in 1732
by her bishop, Dr. Jesper Swedberg, Skara*, the first and
only English translation of which appeared in the *New
Church Magazine* of Boston, in the September and succeed-
ing numbers of 1873-1874.

The bishop lived to the advanced age of eighty-two, fulfilling acceptably all the duties of his Episcopate to the last. His first wife,—he was three times married,—the mother of Emanuel, was Sarah Behm, daughter of Albert Behm, assessor in the college of mines and owner of the extensive mines of Tallfors. The social position occupied by the family, both on the father's and on the mother's side, justify the presumption that their children enjoyed the best educational advantages that Sweden afforded at that period. Of him, as of Samson, it may be said he was born a Nazarite from his mother's womb. In one of his letters to Dr. Beyer, near the close of his life, he said:

"From my fourth to my tenth year I was constantly occupied with thoughts of God, salvation, and the spiritual affections of men; and several times I revealed things at which my father and mother wondered, saying that angels must be speaking through me. From my sixth to my twelfth year, I used to delight in conversing with clergymen about faith, saying that the life of faith is love, and that the love which imparts life is love to the neighbor; also that God gives faith to every one, but that they only receive it who practise that love. I knew of no faith, at that time, than that God is the Creator and Preserver of Nature; that He imparts understanding and a good disposition to men, etc. I knew nothing at that time of that learned faith which teaches that God the Father imputes the righteousness of His Son to whomsoever, and at such times as, He chooses, even to those who have not repented and have not reformed their lives. And had I heard of such a faith it would have been then, as it is now, above my comprehension."

Of his academic life we only know that he was educated at the University of Upsala, and in point of scholarship was admirably equipped for the studies to which he consecrated the rest of his life. He introduced himself to the world in 1709, with a *Selectiou of Sentences from Seneca and Publius Syrus Mimus*, enriched with comments of his own on "*Friendship*" and on other virtues.

II.

1710–1742.

The second period of Swedenborg's life was devoted to the study and the practical application of Natural Science. His rare gifts for mathematics and mechanics soon won for him the favor of the young king Charles XII, the office of Assessor of Mines, and a patent of nobility, with a seat in the upper house of the Swedish Parliament.

On leaving the university, and while preparing for a prolonged sojourn in England, to perfect his education, he revealed, in a letter to his brother-in-law, Benzelius, the bent his mind had already received towards the study of mathematics. " ··· And now at my departure," he wrote, "I propose to myself, gradually to gather and work up a collection *of things discovered and to be discovered in mathematics*, or, what is nearly the same thing, to measure *the progress made in mathematics during the last one or two centuries*. This collection will include all branches of mathematics, and will I trust be of use to me during my journeys."

In his twenty-first year he was sent to England, where on less than $200 a year he spent between two and three years in the prosecution of his favorite study, and its application to the sciences of astronomy and mechanics,— seeking the acquaintance and frequenting the society of those who were presumed to be masters of those sciences. Writing to Benzelius, soon after his arrival in London, he says: "I study Newton daily, and am very anxious to see and hear him." Sir Isaac Newton at this time was in his seventieth year, and president of the Royal Society, of which Sir Hans Sloane was secretary. Swedenborg goes on: "I have provided myself with a small stock of books for the study of mathematics, and also with a certain number of instruments, which are a help in the study of science. I hope that, after settling my accounts, I may have sufficient money left to purchase an air-pump."

He writes again in April following, to Benzelius, who was librarian of the University at Upsala:

"Would you not like to have for the use of the Library a good air-pump, with all the apparatus belonging to it, and the improvements invented by members of the Royal Society? I will send you shortly the books about it, the price and a list of everything belonging to it. Three have been sent to Russia; for there are many Russians here. They mostly study mathematics and navigation, adapting themselves to the taste of their chief, who took a wonderful interest in these subjects during his visit here. The Czar purchased, also, from Mr. Edmund Halley, for eighty pounds, his 'incomparable quadrant,' which he used in discovering the southern stars at St. Helena; and with which he took pretty good observations of the moon and the planets in 1683, 1684, and other years.

.   .   .   .

"I visit daily the best mathematicians here in town. I have been with Flamsteed, who is considered the best astronomer in England, and who is constantly taking observations, which, together with the Paris observations, will give us some day a correct theory respecting the motion of the moon and of its appulse to the fixed stars; and with its help there may be found a true longitude at sea. He has found that the motion of the moon has as yet by no means been well determined; that all theoretical lunar tables are very imperfect; and that the same errors or deviations which are noticed in an earlier period of eighteen years and eleven days, occur again afterwards."

In view of Swedenborg's later career, as a student and teacher of theological science,—upon which his earlier studies must be presumed to have had their influence,—it may not be without profit to read the observations of one of his eminent French contemporaries, upon the judgment passed upon mathematical studies, in which Swedenborg was so proficient, by two of the most popular and illustrious theological teachers of the preceding generation. D'Alembert, in his *Eloge of Bossuet*,[1] says:

"Of all the profane studies, that of mathematics was the only one which the young ecclesiastic believed he

---

[1] *Œuvres de D'Alembert*, vol. 2, p. 247.

had a right to negleƌt; not from contempt of them (we do not fear to say that such a contempt would be a stain upon the memory of the great Bossuet), but because such knowledge did not appear to him of any utility to religion. We might be accused of being at once judges and parties if we dared to appeal from this rigorous proscription. Nevertheless it should be permitted us to observe, all individual interest apart, that the growing theologian did not treat with adequate justice or information a science which is not so useless as he thinks, to the theologian; a science in effeƌt so suitable,—not to correƌt those who are indifferent to the truth (*les esprits faux*), condemned to remain what nature made them, but to fortify, in better natures, that justness so much the more necessary as the subjeƌt of their meditation is more important or more sublime. Could Bossuet be ignorant that the habit of demonstration, in leading us to recognize and seize evidence in everything which is susceptible of proof, teaches us also not to call that demonstration which is not, and to discern the limits which, in the narrow circle of human knowledge, separate daylight from twilight, and twilight from darkness?

"Shall we have the courage to avow here also that the indulgent Fenelon, so unlike Bossuet in other respeƌts, treated mathematics yet more rigorously than he? He wrote in so many words to a young man, whom he direƌted *not to allow himself to be bewitched by the diabolical attraƌtions of geometry, which should extinguish in him the spirit of grace.* Without doubt the arid and severe speculations of this science, which Bossuet accused only of being useless to theology, appeared, to the tender and exalted soul of Fenelon, a poison to those mystic contemplations for which he had but too marked a weakness. But if that was all of geometry's crime, in the eyes of the Archbishop of Cambray, it is difficult to pronounce her guilty."

Whether less mathematics in Swedenborg or more in Bossuet would have modified, to any important extent, their opinions or their influence as religious teachers, is a question about which the greatest diversity of opinion might exist; but it will scarcely be questioned, that a habit of subjecting problems of natural science to the mathematical crucible is calculated to inspire confidence in the conclusions which a mind formed by such a habit is satisfied with.

The fruits of Swedenborg's labors, during what we have termed the second period of his career, are preserved in seventy-seven distinct works, all of which were written in Latin, except twenty in the Swedish tongue. About half of the whole are still in manuscript, the substance of most of them having been incorporated into the larger works which were printed. Though it will not probably be contested, that Swedenborg led all his contemporaries in nearly if not quite the whole range of applied science which he cultivated, his scientific writings are chiefly interesting to the modern reader for the part they had in preparing him for the higher task to which he felt himself called to consecrate the last thirty years of his life. The mere titles of his scientific works are enough to appall the modern student, by the evidence they furnish of his industry and the range of his explorations. They also show that this man, whom the world has been disposed to regard as the most chimerical of dreamers, was the most practical as well as one of the most ingenious of philosophers.

He was the first to introduce into Sweden the differential and integral calculus.

The validity of a patent for the modern air-tight stove, now in such universal use, has been recently contested and set aside in our courts, upon the ground that the principle of the stove was discovered and made known by Swedenborg more than a century ago.

His *Specimens of Chemistry and Physics* contain the germs of the atomic theory set forth afterwards by Dalton.

The French chemist Dumas ascribes to Swedenborg the creation of the modern science of crystallography.

Nineteen years before Franklin's famous experiments, Swedenborg had reasoned out the identity of lightning and electricity.[1]

---

[1] Swedenborg was residing in London during the latter part of Franklin's sojourn in that metropolis, and though it does not appear that either ever at

He anticipated Laplace by more than thirty years in the discovery that the planets and planetary motion are derived from the sun ; and while his hypothesis differs essentially from that of Laplace, it is experimentally illustrated by De. Plateau's celebrated experiment of a rotating fluid mass relieved from the action of gravity.

He also discovered the animation of the brain ; its coincidence during formation with the systole and diastole of the heart, and, after birth, with the respiration of the lungs ; and, incidental to this, the universal motion generated by the lungs and distributed to the whole animal machine.

It is now a well recognized law of physical science, that Action and Reaction are equal, simultaneous and contrary. Prof. Bartlett, late of the United States Military Academy at West Point, nearly a quarter of a century ago, used the above law expressed in a single formula, from which he derived all the consequences of the action of force upon matter. He says[1] (referring to its introduction in 1856) :

tracted the other's notice, or enjoyed his acquaintance, the following letter from Franklin, written in 1788, shows that he was familiar with his illustrious contempory's scientific works, and shared the accepted opinion of their value and practical importance.

Franklin to Benjamin Chambers and others, Chambersburg:

ON THE WATER BLAST FOR FURNACES.

PHILADA., Sept. 20, 1788.

Gentlemen: I received the letter you did me the honor of writing to me, respecting what was supposed a new invention, the blowing of furnaces by a fall of water. Cohen W. Zantzinger delivered me your letter. I told him that I had several books in my library, which described the same contrivance, and have since shewn them to him. They are "The French Encyclopedia, or Dictionary of Arts and Sciences;" *Swedenborg's Latin Treatise on Iron Works,* and the French work *Des Arts et des Meliers,* in the article "Forges." Those descriptions are all accompanied with figures in copper plate, which demonstrate the invention to be the same precisely, in all its essential parts; and in the accounts of it, it is said to have been first practised in Italy, about 100 years since; whence it was brought into France, where it is now much used; thence into Sweden and Germany; and I remember to have been informed by a Spaniard, who was here forty years ago and gave me a drawing of it, that it was practised in some parts of Mexico, in their furnaces for smelting their silver ore. This being the case, you see, gentlemen, that Mr. McClintock cannot properly be recommended to the Assembly, as something new, etc.— *Bigelow's Complete Works of Franklin, under date of Sept. 20, 1788.*

[1] Bartlett's *Analytical Mechanics,* 9th edition.

"That formula was no other than the simple analytical expression of what is now generally called the *law of the conservation of energy*, which has since revolutionized science in nearly all its branches, and which at that time was but little developed or accepted. It is believed that this was not only the first, but that it even still is the only treatise on Analytical Mechanics in which all the phenomena are presented as mere consequences of that single law."

The same law of Action and Reaction, as applied to the moral forces, was stated by Swedenborg more than a century ago,[1] giving us a striking illustration of the universality and simplicity of the law govering both worlds. In its later phase it is an essential part of what the disciples of Swedenborg regard as the most conclusive argument that has yet been made in favor of the freedom of the Will.

Among all the men who rose to eminence in any of the departments of Natural Science during his time, it would be difficult to name one whose labors in the different departments of applied science it would be more interesting or more profitable to dwell upon. They suggest to the most careless reader, what a more careful examination would demonstrate, that the most striking feature of unity that charactrizes them all, from the beginning to the end, and towards which every thing he did, studied, or wrote seemed to tend, was to find the ultimate or final source of power; that force which, both as a philosopher and as an officer of the state, he had been engaged from his youth upward in trying to reduce to the service of

---

[1] "In everything created by God there is reaction. In Life alone there is action; reaction is caused by the action of Life. Because reaction takes place when any created thing is acted upon, it appears as if it belonged to what is created. Thus in man it appears as if the reaction were his, because he has no other feeling than that life is his, when yet man is only a recipient of life. From this cause it is that man, by reason of his hereditary evil, reacts against God. But so far as man believes that all his life is from God, and that all good of life is from the action of God, and all evil of life from the reaction of man, so far his reaction comes to be from [God's] action, and man acts with God as if from himself. The equilibrium of all things is from action and from simultaneous reaction, and everything must be in equilibrium. These things have been said lest man should believe that he himself ascends towards God from himself, and not from the Lord."—Swedenborg's *Divine Love and Wisdom*, n. 68.

mankind ; and to the contemplation and service of which, when found, he consecrated the remainder of his life.[1]

The ability to treat such a variety of topics, and most of them, I may add upon the authority of perfectly competent testimony, as no other man of the time could have treated them, is due to qualities of mind and character which have scarcely received from his biographers the attention they merit. There was no kind of knowledge which could be made useful to his fellow creatures that he thought it beneath him to master, or which he neglected an opportunity of mastering. In one of his letters, dated July 18, 1709, he says:

. . . .

"During my stay here, I have acquired the manual art of binding books ; for we have a book-binder with us ; I have already displayed my skill upon two books, which I bound in half-morocco."

On March 6 following he writes that he had added another accomplishment to that of book-binding:

[1] From an admirable paper on " *Swedenborg as a Scientist*," by Rev. Chauncey Giles, we are tempted to quote the concluding paragraph:

"In conclusion, I know of no element essential to a scientific mind of the highest order which he did not possess. He set out with the noblest ends, the discovery of truth for the glory of God. He pursued them with a patience that never wearied, and a strength that never failed. He planted every step upon the solid basis of experience and fact. He took mathematics, which by many is considered as the only demonstrative and absolute science, for his guide. He used both the methods of analysis and synthesis in every step he took, and by these means he continually rectified his conclusions. He was as docile as a child, and yet was too wise and sharp-sighted to be deceived by appearances. He was not credulous. 'Prove all things, and hold fast the true and good,' was his constant practice. His intellect was eminently constructive. He was ingenious and alert in discovering new methods and applying them. Temperate in his appetites, virtuous in his habits, deaf to applause, devoid of envy or ambition, indefatigable in effort; with an intellect cool and clear as his own sky, a courage that feared nothing but error, a judgment unbiased by opinion or favor and competent to weigh the value of every fact, he worked on with untiring perseverance for more than thirty years, hasting not, resting not in the examination of the material world and the organic forms of the material body. And thus in his life and by his deeds he demonstrated the truth that he possessed a scientific mind second to none and equal to the greatest in any age; and he laid the foundation broad and deep in the material world for his ascent into the higher realms of spiritual knowledge. To his native endowments of docility, intellectual integrity, and devotion to the truth, he added the culture, the strength, the alertness, the courage, and the skill necessary to bring the worlds of spirit and matter together, and in the forms of the lower reveal to man the existence, the reality, the presence, and the perfection of the higher."

For a list of Swedenborg's Literary, Scientific, and Academic writings, see the Supplement, p. lxxix.

"I have little desire to remain here much longer," he says, "for I am wasting most of my time. Still, I have made such progress in music, that I have been able several times to take the place of our organist."

Swedenborg could never see anything done exhibiting ingenuity, or skill, and usefulness, combined, that he did not experience what he described as an "immoderate desire," to master its secret. Writing afterwards from London, he said:

"I also turn my lodgings to some use, and change them often; at first I was at a watchmaker's, and now I am at a mathematical instrument maker's; from them I take their trade, which some day will be of use to me. I have recently computed, for my own pleasure, several useful tables for the latitude at Upsala, and all the solar and lunar eclipses which will take place between 1712 and 1721; I am willing to communicate them if it be desired. In undertaking, in astronomy, to facilitate the calculation of eclipses, and the motion of the moon outside those of the syzygies, and also in undertaking to correct the tables so as to agree with the new observations, I shall have enough to do."

Writing to his brother-in-law in 1712, about some globes that he had been instructed to procure for the Royal Library, he says:

"It is almost impossible to get the paper for the globes; for they are afraid they will be copied. Those that are mounted are, on the other hand, very dear. I have therefore thought of engraving a couple myself, with my own hands,—but only of the ordinary size, ten-twelfths of a Swedish foot,—and after they are done I will send both the drawing and the plates to Sweden. After my return I may perhaps make some of more value. I have already perfected myself so much in the art of engraving that I consider myself capable of it. A specimen of my art I enclose in my father's letter; this, which illustrates some of my inventions, was the first thing I took in hand. At the same time I have learned so much from my landlord, in the art of making brass instruments, that I have manufactured many for my own use. Were I in Sweden, I should not need to apply to any one to make the meridians for the globe, and its other appurtenances.

"With the little *camera obscura*, which you had the kindness to send me, I have already learned perspective drawing to my own satisfaction. I have practiced on churches, houses, etc. If I were among the lifting machines in Fahlun or elsewhere, I could make drawings of them as well as any one else, by means of this little instrument."

Here we have a man perfectly equipped for eminent success in the highest range of philosophical inquiry, who, in the short space of five or six years, makes himself practically acquainted with seven of the industrial arts,— book-binding, music, the manufacture of watches, furniture, and mathematical instruments, engraving, perspective drawing; no one of which in the days of Plato would have been, and scarcely now is, thought a desirable acquisition for a gentleman. At the comparatively early age when these letters were written, Swedenborg was coming, unconsciously, perhaps, under the dominion of the great principle which he lived afterwards to illustrate with singular efficacy, both by precept and example, that the only genuine happiness this life or any other can yield, results from efforts to promote the welfare of others.

When he published his *Opera Philosophica et Mineralia*, in which he gave with considerable detail the theoretical and practical process of copper and iron melting, he was taken to task by others in the business, for revealing its mysteries to the public. Speaking of these censors in one of his letters, he writes:—"There are some who love to hold knowledge for themselves alone, and to be reputed possessors and guardians of secrets. People of this kind grudge the public everything; and if any discovery by which Art and Science will be benefited comes to light, they look at it askance with scowling visage, and probably denounce the discoverer as a babbler, who lets out secrets. Why should secrets be grudged to the public? Why withheld from this enlightened age? Whatever is worth knowing should by all means be brought into the common market of the world. Unless this be done we can neither grow wiser nor happier with time."

It was this early direction of his character and life which made him one of the earliest and most enlightened apostles of popular sovereignty. For his own and his excellent father's public services, his family was ennobled in 1718, and it then took the name of Swedenborg. This gave him a seat in the House of Peers or upper house of the Swedish Parliament, where he exhibited a capacity for statesmanship scarcely inferior to that which made him famous as a philosopher. He was one of the most conspicuous champions of a constitutional government for Sweden, that should set bounds to the whims of a capricious sovereign, and his too unrestricted power. He boldly took the stand to which Hampden and Russell only a few years before had been martyrs,—and which it required great courage, sagacity and virtue to maintain, in any legislative body in the eighteenth century,—that government should be organized and conducted for the good of the governed, and that no man was fit to be entrusted with absolute power. "No one," he said in one of his memorials to the Diet, involving the question of enlarging the prerogatives of the Crown, "No one has the right to leave his life and property in the absolute power of any individual; for of these God alone is master, and we are merely His stewards in this world. . . . I shudder when I reflect what may happen, and probably will happen, if private interests, by which the public good is shoved into the background, should gain the ascendency here. Besides, I cannot see any difference between a king of Sweden who possesses absolute power and an idol; for all turn themselves heart and soul as well to the one as to the other; they obey his will, and worship what passes from his mouth."

During his youth, Swedenborg had witnessed the misfortunes into which an unlimited monarchy had precipitated his country,—the misery and distress of eighteen years of war, with its dearly-bought victories and its bloody defeats, its decimated armies, followed by a bankrupt treasury, pestilence and famine,—and though always a favorite of the king, he never relaxed his efforts, from the day he was clothed with the responsibilities of a legislator, to bring the power and prerogatives of the crown under the supervision and control of the people, or their representatives.   So successful were he and his colleagues in curtailing the royal authority, that when, in 1756, the king refused his signature to measures resolved upon by the Privy Executive Council, he was one of the members of the Diet who empowered the Council to put the royal signature to the bill with a Stamp.

Pausing at Rotterdam in 1736, while on one of his continental excursions, he made a record of his admiration of the republican institutions of Holland, in which he discovered "the surest guarantee of civil and religious liberty, and a form of government more pleasing in the sight of God than that of absolute empire." "In a Republic," he adds, "no undue veneration and homage is paid to any man, but the highest and the lowest deems himself the equal of kings or emperors. . . The only being whom they venerate is God. And where He alone is worshipped, and men are not, is the country most acceptable to Him. . . They do not abase themselves under the influence of shame or fear, but may always preserve a firm, sound mind ; and with a free spirit and erect air may commit themselves and their concerns to God, who alone claims to govern all things. Far otherwise," he continues, "is the case under absolute governments, where men are trained to simulation and deceit ; where they learn to have one thing in their thoughts and another on their tongue ; and where, by long habit, they become inured to what is fictitious and counterfeit, that even in divine worship they speak one thing and think another, and try to palm off upon God their falsity and adulation." This was strong language to use at a time when all Europe, save the small states of Holland and Switzerland, were under the rule, practically, of absolute monarchs.

At a period, too, when every country was trying to pay its debts with a cheaper money than that by which they were incurred, Swedenborg was an impassioned champion of specie payments, a sound currency, and an honest maintenance of all public engagements.   The Count A. J. Von Höpken, for many years prime minister of Sweden while Swedenborg sat in the House of Peers, in a letter to a friend, said of Swedenborg:

"He possessed a sound judgment upon all occasions; he saw everything clearly, and expressed himself well on all subjects. The most solid and the best written memorials presented to the Diet of 1761 on matters of finance were from his pen."

Two or three appeals on this subject have been preserved. One of them closes with the following paragraph:

"If any country could exist by means of a paper currency, which is a substitute for, but is not, money, it would be a country without a parallel."

Swedenborg also labored earnestly in the Diet to check intemperance. On the fly-leaf of one of his books was found the following, in his hand-writing: "The immoderate use of spirituous liquors will be the ruin of the Swedish people." He proposed several measures to the Diet intended to lessen the consumption of spirits, and the waste of grain in their distillation. In order to diminish the number of drunkards, he recommended, in one of his memorials to the Diet, that "all public houses in town should be like bakers' shops, with an opening in the window through which those who desired might purchase whiskey or brandy, without being allowed to enter the house and lounge about in the tap-room."

Another of his propositions, which was adopted by the Diet, was to limit the distillation of whiskey, and to raise it in price by farming out the right of distilling it. "If the distilling of whiskey," he says in his memorial to the Diet, "were farmed out in every judicial district, and also in the towns, to the highest bidder, a considerable revenue might be obtained for the country, and the consumption of grain might also be reduced; that is, if the consumption of whiskey cannot be done away with altogether, which would be more desirable for the country's welfare and morality than all the income which could be realized from so pernicious a drink."

III.

1743–1772.

Before the last important scientific work of Sweden-borg had come from the press, he had an experience so unusual as to be almost unique, that changed the direction and character of his studies for the rest of his life. What this experience was, is best described in his own words. In a brief Autobiography which he prepared, near the close of his eighty-second year, he says:

"But all that I have thus far related, I consider of comparatively little importance ; for it is far transcended by the circumstance that I have been called to a holy office by the Lord Himself, who most mercifully appeared before me, His servant, in the year 1743, when He opened my sight into the spiritual world, and enabled me to con-verse with spirits and angels; in which state I have continued up to the present day. From that time I be-gan to print and publish the various arcana that were seen by me, concerning Heaven and Hell, the State of Man after Death, the True Worship of God, the Spiritual Sense of the Word, and many other important matters conducive to salvation and wisdom."

The same year that he wrote the foregoing, one of the Swedish bishops had given orders for the confiscation of his work *De Amore Conjugiali.* Swedenborg addressed a memorial to the king upon the subject, in which he com-plained, among other things, that he had been treated as no one had ever been treated before in Sweden since the introduction of Christianity; and in the course of his remonstrance he gives a more detailed account of what he regarded as his illumination.

"I humbly beg," he says, "to make the following state-ment:—That our Saviour visibly revealed Himself before me, and commanded me to do what I have done and what I have still to do. And that thereupon He per-mitted me to have intercourse with angels and spirits, I have declared before the whole of Christendom; in Eng-land, Holland, Germany, and Denmark, in France and

Spain, and also on various occasions in this country before
their Royal majesties,—and especially when I enjoyed the
grace to eat at their tables, in the presence of the whole
Royal family, and also of five senators and others; at
which time my mission constituted the sole topic of conversation.   Subsequently, I made this known also to
many senators; and among these, Count Tessin,[1] Count
Bonde[2] and Count Höpken[3] have found it in truth to be
so; and Count Höpken, a gentleman of enlightened understanding, still continues to believe; not to mention
many others, both at home and abroad, among whom are
kings and princes.   All this, however, the Chancellor of
Justice, if public rumor is correct, declares to be false.
Should he reply that the thing is inconceivable to him, I
cannot gainsay it, since I am unable to put the state of
my sight and speech into his head; neither am I able to
cause angels and spirits to converse with him; nor do
miracles happen now.   But his very reason will enable
him to see this when he has thoughtfully read my writings,—wherein much may be found which has never before
been revealed, and which could only be discovered by
actual vision, and intercourse with those who are in the
spiritual world.   In order that reason may see and acknowledge this, I beg that your Majesty may peruse what
has been said on this subject in my book *De Amore Conjugiali*, in a memorable relation on pages 314 to 316.   .   .
If any doubt should still remain, I am ready to testify
with the most solemn oath that may be prescribed to me,
that it is entirely true, a reality without the least fallacy,
that our Saviour permits me to experience this.   It is not
on my own account, but for His interest in the eternal
welfare of all Christians.   Such being the facts, it is wrong
to pronounce them false, though they may be pronounced
incomprehensible."

In a letter addressed in 1771 to the Landgrave of
Hesse-Darmstadt, Swedenborg assigns the reason for his
selection as the channel of this new revelation:

---

[1] President of the House of Nobles and Minister Plenipotentiary to Paris;
founder of the Swedish Academy of Fine Arts.
[2] President of the College of Mines, and Chancellor of the University.
[3] Minister of Foreign Affairs, and President of the Court of Chancery of Upsala.

"In your gracious letter you ask how I came to have intercourse with angels and spirits, and whether this state could be imparted by one to another. Please accept the following reply :

"The Lord our Saviour foretold that he would come again into the world, and institute a New Church. He predicted this in Revelation XXI. and XXII., and also in several places in the Gospels. But as He cannot come again into the world in person, it was necessary that He should do it by means of a man who should not only receive the doctrines of that church in his understanding, but should also publish it by the press ; and as the Lord had prepared me for this from my childhood, He manifested Himself in person before me, His servant, and sent me to do this work. This took place in the year 1743 ; and afterwards He opened the sight of my spirit, and thus introduced me into the spiritual world, granting me to see the heavens, and many wonderful things there, and also the hells, and to talk with angels and spirits,— and this continually for twenty-seven years. This took place with me on account of the church which I mention above, the doctrine of which is contained in my books. The gift of conversing with spirits and angels cannot be transferred from one person to another ; as in my case, the Lord Himself opens the sight of the person. It is sometimes granted to a spirit to enter and communicate with a man ; but leave is not given the man to speak with him mouth to mouth."

But there is no more remarkable nor more satisfactory explanation of his special fitness for his mission, if his own allegations may be accepted in all their length and breadth, than the peculiar and strange competence of his respiratory functions. We are not aware that the faculty of conscious internal as distinct from external respiration, which Swedenborg attributed to himself, was ever before possessed by any man. In a diary of his spiritual experiences, which Swedenborg was accustomed to keep after "the opening of his spiritual vision," occur the following passages :

"I also conversed with them respecting the nature of their speech ; and in order that I might perceive it, the peculiarity of their breathing was shown to me, and I was informed that the breathing of the lungs varies successively, according to the state of their faith. This was unknown to me before, and yet I can perceive and believe it, because my breathing has been so formed by the Lord that for a considerable time I could breathe inwardly, without the aid of the external air, and yet the external senses continue in their vigor. This faculty cannot be possessed by any but those who are so formed by the Lord, and, it is said, not otherwise than miraculously. I was informed also that my breathing is so directed, without my knowledge, in order that I may be with spirits and speak with them. . . I was accustomed to breathe in this way first in my childhood, when praying my morning and evening prayers; sometimes also afterwards, when I was exploring the concordance of the lungs and the heart; and especially when I was writing from my mind the things which have been published for many years. I observed, constantly, that there was a tacit breathing, hardly sensible,—about which it was afterwards given me to think, and then to write. Thus was I introduced into such breathings from infancy onward through many years; and afterwards, when heaven was opened to me, so that I might converse with spirits, I scarcely inhaled at all for more than an hour,—only just enough air to enable me to think. So I was introduced into interior respiration by the Lord."

If, as Swedenborg asserts, this faculty of internal respiration for a time without the aid of the external air, can only be possessed by those who are so formed by the Lord, and, as he was told,—he does not aver the fact of his own knowledge,—miraculously, it is a matter which human science necessarily has difficulty in taking jurisdiction of. It has, however, provoked some very interesting and striking reflections from Dr. Wilkinson, an eminent physician of London, author of an eloquent biography of Swedenborg, and translator of some of his most important scientific works.

"As we breathe," he says, "so we are. Inward thoughts have inward breaths, and purer spiritual thoughts have spiritual breaths hardly mixed with material. Death is breathlessness. Fully to breathe the external atmosphere is equivalent, *cæteris paribus*, to living in plenary enjoyment of the senses and the muscular powers.

"On the other hand, the condition of trances or death-life is the persistence of the inner breath of thoughts, or the soul's sensation, while the breath of the body is annulled. It is only those in whom this can have place, that may still live in this world and yet be consciously associated with the persons and events in the other. Hybernation and other phenomena come in support of these remarks. Thus we have common experience on our side in asserting, that the capacities of the inward life, whether thought, meditation, contemplation or trance, depend upon those of the respiration.

"Some analogous power over the breath, a power to live and think without respiring,—for it is the bodily respiration that draws down the mind at the same time that it draws up the air, and thus causes mankind to be compound, or spiritual and material beings,—some analogous power, we say, has lain at the basis of the gifts of many other seers besides Swedenborg.

"It is quite apparent that the Hindu Yogi were capable of similiar states; and in our day, the phenomena of hypnotism have taught us much in a scientific manner of these ancient conditions and sempiternal laws. Take away or suspend that which draws you to this world, and the spirit by its own lightness floats upwards into the other. There is, however, a difference between Swedenborg's state, as he reports it, and the modern instances, inasmuch as the latter are artificial and induced by external effort, whereas Swedenborg's was natural and we may say congenital; was the combined regime of his aspirations and his respirations; did not engender sleep, but was accompanied by full waking and open eyes; and was not courted in the first instance for the trances and the visions that it brought. Other cases, moreover, are occasional, whereas Swedenborg's appears to have been uninterupted, or nearly so, for twenty-seven years." . .

"To show how intelligent Swedenborg was of these deep things, we have only to examine his anatomical works and manuscripts, which present a regular progress of ideas on the subject of respiration. 'If we carefully attend to profound thought,' he says, 'we shall find that when we *draw breath* a host of ideas rush from beneath, as through an open door, into the sphere of thought; whereas when we hold the breath and slowly let it out we deeply keep the while in the tenor of our thought, and communicate as it were with the higher faculty of the soul,—as I have observed in my own person times out of number. Retaining or holding back the breath is equivalent to having intercourse with the soul; attracting or drawing it amounts to intercourse with the body.'

"This indeed is a fact so common that we never think about it; so near to natural life that its axioms are almost too substantial for knowledge. Not to go so profound as to the intellectual sphere, we may remark that all fineness of bodily work,—all that in art which comes out of the infinite delicacy of manhood as contrasted with animality, requires a corresponding breathlessness and expiring. To listen attentively to the finest and least obtrusive sounds, as with the stethoscope to the murmurs in the breast, or with mouth and ear to distant sounds, needs a hush that breathing disturbs; the common ear has to die and be born again to exercise these delicate attentions.

"To take an aim at a rapidly flying or minute object, requires in like manner a breathless time and a steady act. The very pulse must receive from the stopped lungs a pressure of calm. To adjust the exquisite machinery of watches, or other instruments, requires in the manipulator a motionless power of his own central springs. Even to see and observe, with an eye like the mind itself, necessitates a radiant pause. Again, for the negative proof: We see that the first actions and attempts of children are unsuccessful, being too quick, and full moreover of confusing breaths; the life has not fixed aereal space to play the game, but the scene itself flaps and flutters with alien wishes and thoughts. In short, the whole reverence of remark and deed depends upon the above conditions, and we lay it down as a general truth, that every man requires to educate his breath for his business. Bodily strength, mental strength, even wisdom, all lean upon our respirations; and Swedenborg's case is but a striking instance, raising to a very visible size a fact which, like the air, is felt and wanted, but for the most part not perceived."

The respect which so acute and accomplished a physiologist as Dr. Wilkinson testifies for this pretension of Swedenborg, encourages me to add a remark which may find ample confirmation in every one's experience; it is, that those whose habits and vocation in life involve the most active employment of what Swedenborg terms the external respiratory organs, are as a rule least disposed to the study and contemplation of spiritual forces. They were styled the Bœotians among the Greeks, and "their talk was of bullocks," among the Hebrews.

Swedenborg believed that his studies in Natural Science had been one of the important agencies by which he had been prepared for his sacred office.

"What' the acts of my life involved," he wrote, "I could not distinguish at the time they happened; but by the Divine mercy of God-Messiah I was afterwards informed with regard to some, even many, particulars. From these I was at last able to see that the Divine Providence immediately governed the acts of my life from my youth, and so directed them that by means of knowledge of natural things I was enabled to reach a state of intelligence, and thus, by the Divine mercy of God-Messiah, to serve as an instrument for laying open the things which are hidden interiorly in the Word of God-Messiah. These things are therefore now made manifest, which hitherto were not manifest."[1]

When asked the question, "Why did the Lord reveal the long list of arcana which you have just enumerated to you, who are a layman, and not to one of the clergy?" he replied:

"This was in the good pleasure of the Lord, who had prepared me for this office from my earliest youth. But let me ask you a question: Why did the Lord when He was on earth, choose fishermen for His disciples, and not some of the Lawyers, Scribes, Priests or Rabbis? Con-

[1] *Adversaria*, Part II., No. 839.

sider this well, draw your conclusions correctly, and you will discover the reason."

From the time Swedenborg claims to have been in direct communication with the spiritual world, he abandoned his study of Natural Science and devoted himself for the remaining thirty years of his life, exclusively to the work of writing, arranging and publishing the truths which he believed he received directly from the Lord, and the promulgation of which he understood to mark the advent of the New Church foretold in the Apocalypse.[1] Finding his duties as Assessor incompatible with the work to which he felt himself called, he applied to the king to be relieved from them. The immediate occasion for this application was the death of Councillor Bergenstierna, and a unanimous recommendation from the College of Mines that Assessor Swedenborg should be promoted to his place. In a letter to the king he prays his Majesty to make another selection, and most ·graciously release him from office altogether. He then goes on to add another request :

STOCKHOLM, June 2, 1747.

.   .   .   .

"But as I have been for more than thirty years an Assessor in your Royal Majesty's College of Mines, and have at my own expense made several journeys abroad, to visit mines and other places, and as I have printed there several works for the benefit of my country, for which I have never yet asked the least recompense from the public, but, on the contrary,—that I might be able to devote myself uninterruptedly to these objects,—have given up half my salary, which during the last eleven years, has amounted to upwards of 20,000 rix-dollars in copper, I therefore entertain the hope that you will graciously grant my request, and allow me to continue to draw the half of my salary, as I have been doing. I have less doubt that you will grant this request, because I have performed the duties of an Assessor for more than thirty years, and as well as I can remember, no favor has ever been denied me.

[1] "See Revelation, Chap. XXI."

"It is, therefore, my humble wish, that you graciously release me from office, but without bestowing upon me any higher rank, which I most earnestly beseech you not to do. I further pray, that I may receive half of my salary, and that you will graciously grant me leave to go abroad, to some place where I may finish the important work on which I am now engaged."

The king, by royal decree, acceded both requests, and in the most flattering terms. "Although," he said, "we would gladly see him continue at home the faithful services he has hitherto rendered to us and to his country, still, we can the less oppose his wish, as we feel assured that the work on which he is engaged will, in time, contribute to the public good, not less than the other valuable works written and published by him have contributed to the use and honor of his country, as well as of himself. . . As a token of the satisfaction with which we look upon his long and faithful services, we also most graciously permit him to retain for the rest of his life the half of his salary as an Assessor."

This left Swedenborg financially independent, and completely master of his time ; a condition fatal to the usefulness of a large portion of mankind, but one which is indispensible to the highest order of human achievement. No one can do the greatest things nor even his best in working for himself.

The human mind is, no doubt providentially, equipped with a wise mistrust of all pretensions to supernatural, or exclusive knowledges of any sort. It is a mistrust which protects us from the acceptance of much that is absurd and pernicious. This mistrust, however, like all our faculties of moral selection, if abused, conducts to errors as grave as those from which it is designed to protect us. Reckless scepticism is as misleading as reckless credulity. Whether Swedenborg was actually called to the exalted mission to which he professed and no doubt believed himself to have been called, is a question which there is no occasion here to discuss, but it is proper to say that his pretensions are not to be rejected upon any presumptive impossibility.

Why one man is made a vessel of honor and another of

dishonor is a question which is best answered, perhaps, in
the language of St. Gregory. *Qui in faƐlis Dei rationem
non videt, infirmitatem suam considerans non videat, rationem non videt.*[1]

Has any special messenger of Divine truth of whom
there is any record, ever been received by the children of
men with less mistrust, denounced with less violence, or
endured less persecution than he? Moses, the prophets,
Christ, and His apostles, were all in turn treated more
or less as public enemies, whose teachings threatened the
peace of society. Divine truth always brings to the average man, not peace but the sword. Every stage of our
spiritual growth is the fruit of a combat and a victory
over some prejudice, passion, or unhallowed propensity.
If Moses was denounced by his followers for leading them
into the wilderness to starve ; if the prophets were stoned ;
if Paul and Peter were imprisoned and Christ crucified for
teaching strange doƐtrines, it is not to be presumed that
any new torch-bearer of spiritual light would be wel-
comed by those who are accustomed to dwell in the darkness which such a light was designed to dispel. On the
contrary, a prompt, cheerful, popular acceptance of what
purported to be a new revelation from heaven, would be
tolerably conclusive evidence that it was spurious. Nor
is there any more reason to suppose that all the light
from heaven that was designed for the children of men
had reached them before the birth of Swedenborg, than
that it had reached them before the birth of the Apostles.
It is the Christian belief that God has revealed and will
continue to reveal Himself to His children according to
their necessities. "The apostolical fathers[2] Barnabas,
Clement and Hermas (whose writings were reverenced as of
canonical authority for four hundred years, and were read
with the canonical Scriptures in many of the churches)
confirm the truth that prophecy, divine visions, and miracu-
lous gifts continued in the Church after the Apostolic Age,
both by their testimony and experience ; and to pass over

[1] He who does not see the reason for the aƐts of God, because of his infirm-
ity, does not see the reason for his not seeing it.
[2] Preface to Dr. Hartley's translation of Swedenborg's treatise on *Heaven and
Hell.*

many other venerable names (among whom Tertullian and Origen are witnesses to the same truth afterwards), Euse- bius, Cyprian, Lactantius, still lower down, declare that extraordinary divine manifestations were not uncommon in their days. Cyprian is very express on this subject, prais- ing God on that behalf, with respect to himself, to divers of the clergy and many of the people, using these words : "The discipline of God over us never ceases by night and by day to correct and reprove ; for not only by visions of the night, but also by day, *even the innocent age of children among us is filled with the Holy Spirit, and they see and hear and speak in ecstasy, such things as the Lord vouch- safes to admonish and instruct us by.*" Epist. Rom. 16.

"Where there is no vision," says the Wise man, "the people perish." And therefore it is promised in Joel that the Lord's Spirit shall be upon all flesh in the latter days : "Your sons and your daughters shall prophesy, your old men shall dream dreams, and your young men shall see visions. And also upon the servants and upon the hand- maids in those days will I pour out my Spirit." What else did Joseph mean or claim for himself, when he said to his humiliated brethren : "Wot ye not that such a man as I can certainly divine ?"

No evidence as to personal character of the author could establish a new system of theology, though it might go a long way towards overthrowing one. Nor will it be pretended that the average clergy of any sect or denomination have furnished any higher evidence of their call to be the special interpreters of God's love to men than we find in the life and work of Swedenborg. But it is pertinent to the subject in hand to say, that of the vast army of Christian clergy throughout the world there are comparatively few who on taking orders have not solemnly proclaimed their conviction that they were "called to the order and ministry of the priesthood by the will of our Lord Jesus Christ." This language may, to a certain extent, have degenerated into a formula, but it once expressed a dogmatic conviction, that the ministers of Christ's church were called in the same way, to the same uses, and by the same voices as the apostles had been called. Whether Swedenborg did hear the Saviour's knock and open the door, whether he did hold the commission and receive the instructions he professes to have received, are questions which cannot be determined by the testimony of Swedenborg; for though there was never probably a more truthful man, nor one who lived more exclusively to the honor and glory of God, he was human and therefore liable to illusions; neither can these questions be determined by other witnesses, because from the nature of the case, there were and could have been none.

They must be determined, if at all, by the character of the communications he professes to have received. If they seem to be of sufficient importance to justify their alleged divine origin; if they harmonize at all points with the record which all Christians accept as the genuine Word of God; if they make the Word plainer; if they reconcile things in the Word which before seemed inconsistent, and tend to unite those who before were divided in regard to its teachings, then it would be unreasonable to suppose that Swedenborg was the victim of illusions, and did not enjoy the intercourse with our Lord and the angels which he professed and believed he enjoyed.

From the period of his alleged illumination in 1743-5 to his death in 1772, a period of nearly thirty years, Swedenborg wrote very voluminously. Apart from one or two scientific works, then just completed, he published scarcely a line that was not written under what he regarded as direct instruction from the Lord. What he published during this period comprehends his entire system of theology and hermeneutics, and occupies some thirty volumes.[1]

The conviction of a personal calling by the Lord, and of enjoying continuous association with His angels for nearly thirty years, is an experience, so far as we know, without precedent; and the fruits of such experience, to whatever cause we may ascribe it, can never cease to be an interesting and profitable study. Some notion of the fertility of his pen, and of the subjects which occupied it during these latter years of his life, may be gathered from a glance at the titles of his various printed works, and of his unpublished manuscripts that are preserved.

---

[1] Now published by the American Swedenborg Printing and Publishing Society, at the Cooper Union, in nineteen volumes.

The doctrines taught by Swedenborg which nave thus far left the most distinct impression upon the theology of the world probably are :

1. The doctrine of the Lord, and incidentally of the Redemption and Atonement, by which the unity of God is reconciled to human reason with His trinity, of Father, Son and Holy Spirit.

2. The doctrine of the future life, by which the existence of the hells is reconciled with the infinite love of God, which, as he maintains, is as continually and abundantly manifested over the inhabitants of the hells as over the inhabitants of the heavens.

3. The doctrine of the Sacred Scripture, and of correspondences, by which the plenary inspiration, divinity, and holiness of the Word are rationally established ; its apparent incongruities and inconsistencies explained, and reconciled to human intelligence ; its divine structure vindicated, and its authority exalted.

Swedenborg taught that the Word, or most of what is popularly termed the Bible, was written, not upon the structural principle of a mere secular history or treatise, but according to a law of correspondence between the natural objects and phenomena described in the Bible, and spiritual truths in which they had their origin, and which they represent. He taught that all causes are spiritual, and that all natural phenomena are but sensual manifestations, or, as he commonly styled them, "ultimates," of some preceding spiritual cause ; that a people having a perception of correspondences,—as he represents the inhabitants of the heavenly world to have, and as he avers that men on earth once had,—when they read of mountains, rivers, lambs, wolves, wars, the deluge, honey, frankincense, or any natural objects or events, perceive not so much the physical objects and external circumstances that appear to the mere outward apprehension, but the spiritual conditions, things or circumstances with which they correspond ; just as when we see a pleasant smile or censorious frown, our attention is occupied with the state of feeling towards us which such smile or frown corresponds to and represents. So there are certain expressions of the face which indicate, to the most careless observer, well defined qualities of character. One, we say, is cunning, another is open and ingenuous, a third is vain, a fourth cruel, a fifth is refined and gentle, and a sixth is sensual and gross. These expressions have been developed on the face, by the exercise and indulgence through life of the several qualities of cunning, of frankness, of vanity, of cruelty, of refinement, or of sensuality. The features *correspond* with the emotions which they respectively reflect or represent.[1]

So the physical phenomena and outward events, etc., which represent the various degrees, shades and varieties of good and evil, of truth and falsity, were used in the composition of the Bible as the most universal means of making the treatment of these subjects edifying to the children of men of every age, in their varying states of spiritual darkness; and as involving a depth and comprehensiveness of meaning capable, by Divine evolution, of meeting the increasing capacity and wants of men in every stage of their upward development and future enlightenment and intelligence, in this world and in the spiritual world.

"All nature and each individual thing in nature," says Swedenborg, "has its spiritual correspondence; and in like manner each and all things in the human body. But hitherto it has been unknown what correspondence is. Yet it was very well known in the most ancient times; for to those who then lived, the knowledge of correspondences was the knowledge of knowledges, and was so universal that all their books and manuscripts were written by correspondences. The Book of Job, which is a book of the Ancient church, is full of correspondences. The hieroglyphics of the Egyptians, and the fabulous stories of highest antiquity were nothing else.

"Also the tabernacle, with all things therein, as well

---

[1] The poet Spenser formulated the whole doctrine of correspondence in the following lines, written two hundred years before Swedenborg made of it a science.

"So every Spirit, as it is most pure,
And hath in it the more of heavenly light,
So it the fairer bodie doth procure
To habit in, and it more fairely dight
With chearful grace and amiable sight;
For of the Soule the bodie forme doth take;
For Soule is forme, and doth the bodie make."

as their feasts,—such as the feast of unleavened bread, the feast of tabernacles, the feast of first-fruits ;—and the priesthood of Aaron and the Levites, and their garments of holiness; and besides these, all their statutes and judgments, which related to their worship and life, were correspondences. Now, since Divine things present themselves in the world by correspondences, therefore the Word was written by pure correspondences. For the same reason the Lord, as He spake from the Divine spake by correspondences; for whatever is from the Divine descends into such things in nature as correspond to the Divine, and which then conceal things Divine, which are called celestial and spiritual, in their bosom."

"Without the spiritual sense," says he in another place, "no one could know why the Prophet Jeremiah was commanded to buy himself a girdle and put it on his loins, and not to draw it through the waters, but to hide it in the hole of a rock by the Euphrates (Jer. xiii. 1–7) or why the Prophet Isaiah was commanded to loose the sackcloth from off his loins, and put off the shoe from off his foot, and to go naked and barefoot three years (Isaiah xx. 2, 3); or why the Prophet Ezekiel was commanded to pass a razor upon his head and upon his beard, and afterwards to divide [the hairs of] them and burn a third part in the midst of the city, smite a third part with the sword, scatter a third part in the wind, and bind a little of them in his skirts, and at last to cast them into the midst of the fire (Ezek. vi. 4); or why the same prophet was commanded to lie upon his left side three hundred and ninety days, and upon his right side forty days; and to make him a cake of wheat and barley and millet and fitches, with cow's dung, and eat it, and in the mean time to raise a rampart and a mound against Jerusalem and besiege it (Ezek. iv. 1–5); or why the Prophet Hosea was twice commanded to take to himself a harlot to wife (Hosea i. 2–9, iii. 2, 3); and many such things. Moreover, who, without the spiritual sense, would know what is signified by all things belonging to the tabernacle,—by the ark, the mercy-seat, the cherubim, the candle-stick, the altar of incense, the bread of faces on the table, and its veils and curtains? Or who, without the spiritual sense, would know what is signified by Aaron's garments of holiness,—by his coat, his cloak, his ephod, the Urim and Thummim, the mitre and other things? Who, without the spiritual sense, would know what is signified by all the things which were enjoined concerning burnt-offerings, sacrifices, meat-offerings and drink-offerings? concerning Sabbaths also, and feasts? *The truth is, that not the least thing of these was enjoined which did not signify something relating to the Lord, to heaven and to the church.* From these few examples it may be clearly seen that there is a spiritual sense in each and all the particulars of the Word."

Swedenborg does not accord precisely the same degree of authority to all the books of the Bible.

"The books of the Word," he says, "are all those that have an internal sense; and those that have not are not of the Word. The books of the Word in the Old Testament are the five books of Moses, the book of Joshua, the book of Judges, the two books of Samuel, the two books of the Kings, the Psalms of David, the Prophets, Isaiah, Jeremiah, the Lamentations, Ezekiel, Daniel, Hosea, Joel, Amos, Obadiah, Jonah, Micah, Nahum, Habakkuk, Zephaniah, Haggai, Zechariah, Malachi; and in the New Testament, the four Evangelists, Matthew, Mark, Luke, John, and the Apocalypse." (*A. C.*, n. 10,325.)

The Book of Genesis, from its beginning to the call of Abram (chapters i.-xl.), says Swedenborg, was not written by Moses, but is a fragment of an older Scripture; neither are those early chapters matter-of-fact history, but compositions, in the form of history, symbolical of things celestial and spiritual.

"They who do not think beyond the sense of the letter, cannot believe otherwise than that the Creation described in the first and second chapters of Genesis means the creation of the universe; and, that within six days heaven and earth and sea, and things therein, and men in the likeness of God, were created; but who, if he ponder deeply, cannot see, that the creation of the universe is not there meant. Common-sense might teach, that the operations there described were impossible; as, that there were days, and light and darkness, and green herbs and fruitful trees before the appearance of the sun and moon. Similiar difficulties follow, which are scarcely credited by any one who thinks interiorly : as, that the Woman was built from the rib of the Man ; that two trees were set in Paradise, and the fruit of one forbidden to be eaten ; that the Serpent discoursed with the Wife of the Man, who was the wisest of mortals, and deceived them both ; and that the universal human race was on that account condemned to Hell.

"Nevertheless it is to be noted, that all things in that story; even to the smallest iota, are divine, and contain in them arcana, which before the angels in the heavens are manifest as in a clear day."[1]

In these eleven allegorical chapters Swedenborg professes to have discovered the history of two Dispensations. The first he designates the Most Ancient Church, and the time of its existence, the Golden Age; the second, the Ancient Church, and the time of its existence, the Silver Age.

The rise of the Most Ancient Church he finds symbolized in the story of Creation ; its culmination, in Adam and Eve in Eden ; its decline in the events following the eating of the tree of the knowledge of good and evil ; and its destruction in the deluge.

The story of the Ancient Church begins with Noah, and is continued in his posterity ; its ruin is depicted in the erection of the Tower of Babel, the confusion of the tongues of the builders and their dispersion over the earth.

A third regime commences, he tells us, with the call of Abram, or rather with Eber, at which point the allegorical style of narration terminates.

That there was a more ancient Word is proved by the allusions in Numbers xxi. 14, and Joshua x. 13, to the *Book of the Wars of Jehovah* and to the *Book of Jasher*. In the Word are three senses or meanings,—the celestial, the spiritual, and the natural or literal. These three senses make one by correspondence.

"With regard to the writings of St. Paul, and the

---

[1] *Arcana Cœlestia*, No. 8891.

other Apostles," he says, "I have not given them a place
in my *Arcana Cœlestia,* because they are dogmatic writings merely, and not written in the style of the Word
like those of the Prophets, of David, of the Evangelists, and the Revelation of St. John. The style of the
Word consists throughout of correspondences, and thereby
effeċts immediate communication with heaven; but the
style of these dogmatic writings is quite different, having
indeed communication with heaven, but only mediate or
indireċt. The reason why the Apostles wrote in this style
was that the Christian Church was then to begin through
them; and the style that is used in the Word would not
have been suitable for such doċtrinal tenets, which required
plain and simple language, adapted to the capacities of all
readers. Nevertheless, the writings of the Apostles are
excellent books for the Church; since they insist on the
doċtrine of charity, and thence faith,—as the Lord Himself has done in the Gospels and in the Revelation of St.
John; which will clearly appear to any one who studies
these writings with attention."[1]

Swedenborg avers that in their highest state of excel-
lence, in the Church before the flood, men had an intuitive
perception of the correspondences that universally exist
in nature, so that their language was the language of nature, that is, of correspondences; and that consequently
the rites of the Church became correspondential, and rep-
resentative of heavenly things; but that in time men became sensual and lost their perception of correspondences,
and the rites of the Church lost, in their minds, their rep-
resentative charaċter. In observing the rites irrespeċtive
of the spiritual things they represented, they at length
became idolatrous.

To recover this lost knowledge of correspondences, he
claims that a new revelation from the Lord was necessary;
that, for reasons which he assigns, he was seleċted as the
medium through which that revelation was to be made,—
at the time, and at the earliest time when the world was
prepared to receive and profit by it; just as the Apostles,
Moses and the prophets were severally and at different

[1] Letter to Dr. Beyer; also *A. C.,* n. 815.

periods of human history, selected for their respective offices. Swedenborg's own testimony upon this subject, already cited, is very remarkable. Nor did he shrink from re-asserting his Divine commission on all suitable occasions.

He says in the *True Christian Religion,* no. 1779: "I testify in truth that the Lord manifested Himself to me His servant, and sent me to this office ; and that afterwards He opened the sight of my spirit and so intromitted me into the spiritual world, and has granted me to see the heavens and the hells, and also to converse with angels and spirits, and this now continually for many years ; likewise that from the first day of that calling I have not received anything whatever relating to the doctrines of that Church from any angel, but from the Lord alone while I was reading the Word."

Again, in the *Apocalypse Explained,* no. 1183, he says: "It has been given me to perceive distinctly what comes from the Lord and what from angels ; what has come from the Lord has been written, and what from the angels has not been written."

In his *Invitation to the New Church* he says also : "The things related by me are not miracles, but are proofs that for certain ends I have been introduced by the Lord into the spiritual world."

One might suspect this to be the language of a madman, perhaps, but not that of an impostor.

It was from the Lord directly, therefore, that Swedenborg claims to have received new light in regard to the interior meaning of the Word, and the key to the correspondence between its letter and its Spirit. The chief results of these communications or revelations were recorded in three distinct works.

The *first,* entitled *Arcana Cœlestia,*[1] appeared in eight quarto volumes, between the years 1749 and 1756, at the rate of about one volume a year, and was consecrated to an exposition of the internal or Spiritual Sense of the

---

[1] *Arcana Cœlestia quæ in Scriptura Sacra, seu in Verbo Domini sunt, detecta ; una cum mirabilibus, quæ visa sunt in Mundi Spirituum et cœlo Angelorum.* This work appeared without the name of the author, or the publisher, or of the place where published.

books of Genesis and Exodus. Each sentence is taken up in its order, and its spiritual import laid open; for Swedenborg maintained that "there is not an iota or apex or little twirl of the Hebrew letters which does not involve something Divine." "This," he says, "has been shown to me from Heaven ; but I know it transcends belief."[1]

Second. The *Apocalypse Revealed*, wherein are uncovered the mysteries there foretold which have hitherto remained concealed.[2]

Third. The *Apocalypse Explained*, wherein are disclosed the mysteries there foretold, which have hitherto remained concealed.[3] The former is more summary, and the latter a more extended work, involving incidentally an exposition of a very considerable part of the rest of the Word.

"This year," says Swedenborg in a letter to his friend Oetinger, writing from Stockholm, Sept. 23, 1766, "there has been published the *Apocalypsis Revelata*, which was promised in the treatise on *The Last Judgment*, and from which it may be clearly seen that I converse with angels; for not the smallest verse in the Apocalypse can be understood without revelation. Who can help seeing that by the New Jerusalem a New Church is meant, and that its doctrines can only be revealed by the Lord,—because they are described there by merely typical things, *i. e.*, by Correspondences ; and likewise that these can be published to the world only by means of some one to whom the revelation has been granted? I can solemnly bear witness that the Lord Himself appeared to me, and that He sent me to do that which I am now doing ; and that for this purpose He has opened the interiors of my mind, which are those of my spirit, so that I can see the things which are in the spiritual world, and hear those who are there ; which [privilege] I have had now for twenty-two years. The mere bearing witness, however, does not suf-

---

[1] *Arc. Cælestia*, no. 9049.

[2] *Apocalypsis Revelata in qua deteguntur arcana quæ ibi prædicta sunt, et hactenus recondita latuerunt.* Amsterdam, 1766, 4to, pp. 629.

[3] *Apocalypsis Explicata secundum sensum spiritualem ubi revelantur Arcana quæ ibi prædicta et hactenus recondita fuerent Ex operibus posthumis Emanuelis Swedenborgii.* Londoni, in 4 vols., 4to, vol. 1, 1785; vol. 2, 1786; vol. 3, 1788; vol. 4, 1789.

ice at the present day to convince men of this; but any
one of a sound understanding may be confirmed by the
testimony of my writings, and especially by the *Apocalypsis Revelata*. Who has heretofore known anything
about the spiritual sense of the Word; and about the
spiritual world, or heaven and hell; or about man's life
after death? Should these, and many other things, be
perpetually hidden from Christians? They have now for
the first time been disclosed for the sake of the New
Church, which is the New Jerusalem, that they [its mem-
bers] may know them; others indeed shall also know
them, who yet do not know them on account of their unbelief."

The *Apocalypse Explained* was discontinued at the
tenth verse of the 19th chapter of the Apocalypse, for
reasons never explained. This and the *Apocalypse Revealed* give what purports to be a complete exposition of
the interior or spiritual significance of the one book of the
Bible which, if Swedenborg's attempt was not a success, has
most effectually defied all human interpretation. Whatever may have been the source of his light, his exposition
is certainly the most intelligible, complete, harmonious
and self-demonstrating of which I have any knowledge.
The three works I have named, embracing in all thirteen
quarto volumes in their original Latin editions, contain
incidentally, besides the explanation of the books to
which they are immediately devoted, an exposition of a
large part of the other books of the Sacred Scriptures,
and the key, moreover, which, according to Swedenborg,
will unlock the hidden treasures of the Word, and without which they might have remained for an indefinite
period, if not forever, inaccessible.

There will continue to be differences of opinion among
men in regard to the sources of Swedenborg's authority
or what he tells us about the spiritual world, the internal
meaning of the Word, and the principles upon which it
was written; just as there will continue to be differences
of opinion in regard to the sources from whence the writers of the Pentateuch, the Prophecies, the Gospels and
the Apocalypse, received what they left us. When our
Lord was walking among men, His pretensions to speak

by Divine authority were generally treated with derision.
Of course, therefore, Swedenborg's testimony,—highly as
it would have been estimated by his contemporaries upon
any subject which only involved his personal probity,
honor, and general intelligence,—would go but a very
short way in support of his pretensions to a supernatural
mission. His writings must prove themselves. His theory
of interpreting the Bible must harmonize so completely
that, to whatever part applied, there shall be no conflict.
And not only must the external or material objects and
incidents in the Bible have the same spiritual meaning
wherever they occur, but those meanings must harmonize
with the obvious and undisputed teachings of the Word
itself.

This harmony is claimed for Swedenborg's teachings
by his more diligent students. They insist that his state-
ment of the correspondences between the letter and the
spirit of the Word, as recorded in Genesis or Exodus, or
in the Apocalypse, and elsewhere, are equally applicable
to the same objects or phenomena in any other part of
the Sacred Scriptures. In other words, that the Word of
God is written as it were in two languages, one natural
or external, the other spiritual or internal; the natural or
external objects or events described having been selected
exclusively because of their spiritual meaning, and having
that meaning in all cases where they appear; even "as
the new wine is found in the cluster, and one saith destroy
it not, for a blessing is in it."

It is but just here to say that Swedenborg does not
profess to give all the internal meaning of which the Word
is the repository. So far from it, he represents the Word
to be infinite; to contain even profounder depths of wisdom than can be expressed in the language of men;
adapted, by successive unfoldings, to the angels of all the
heavens,—to the highest state of intelligence that finite
minds can ever, to all eternity, attain; and extending
upwards even to God Himself, as the rays of light ex-
tend to the sun. In other words, that it is in the true
sense of the term Divine, and therefore infinite. Hence
the necessity that the natural language of the Bible
should be that of correspondences, capable of involving

these hidden things, and so of being adapted to every spiritual state of men on earth and in the heavens. Swedenborg would therefore claim that the highest evidence of the Divine authority of the Bible is to be found in the marvellous light of the manifold but harmonious meanings inhabiting its letter, which the devout and reverent-minded may find revealed through the knowledge of its correspondences now again made known. He teaches, too, that nature is a similar treasury of Divine wisdom, and capable of similar unfoldings,—a vast, continuous series of cause and effect within cause and effect, extending up to God Himself. So that His revealed or written Word and His Word in Nature alike descend from Him, and lead up to Him, who is the inmost and animating soul of both ; not a mere undefined pervading influence, but a Divine Personal God,—an infinitely glorious Divine Man, the great Archetype, of which man was created the finite image.

While there are many to whom Swedenborg's writings have proved unintelligible, just as many fail to discern in the phenomena of their own daily experience an uninterrupted manifestation of God's infinite love and goodness ; while there are many whose minds are never disturbed by those doubts and difficulties which tend to drag their victims out into the dark sea of skepticism and moral chaos ; there is a class which in this age of applied science has been multiplying throughout the Christian world with fearful rapidity, for whom the writings of Swedenborg seem to have a providential mission. To those whose education and training have made it necessary for them to have a reason for the faith that is in them; who are too conscientious to profess a belief in statements which they cannot reconcile with their experience or their reason ; who think the human intellect is fully competent to measure and appropriate all the truth of which man has need in this life, Swedenborg has brought unspeakable comfort and satisfaction, by letting them see that they were the victims of their own blindness rather than, as they had allowed themselves to suppose, of the obscurity of the Scriptures. Of the already large number of this class who owe to the writings of Swedenborg the restoration of their impaired

faith in the Divine authority of the Word, the writer grate
fully acknowledges himself to be one. It has also been
his good fortune to know of many others who have been
delivered from the bonds of dreary and hopeless unbelief
by touching the hem of the same garment. The waters
of Abana and Parphar may be better than all the rivers of
Damascus for some purposes, but not for all.

IV.

Swedenborg was rather above middle height, and very
active, even in old age. His hair was of a pale auburn
color, and his eyes of a brownish grey. In his youth he
was thought handsome, and his face, always full of be-
nevolence and tenderness, retained unequivocal traces of
beauty till his death. When in his eighty-first year, he
told a friend that he then had a new set of teeth growing
in his mouth. Flaxman the eminent sculptor, who exam-
ined Swedenborg's skull after death, said, "a cast ought
to be taken of it, if only for its beauty."

Swedenborg was never married. While associated
with Councillor Polhem, "the great Swedish Archimedes,"
as Swedenborg called him, in the construction of the
locks at the outlet of Lake Wenner, and residing in his
family, he became enamored of one of the Councillor's
daughters; and not only the father, but the king became
interested in his suit, the latter desiring thereby to bind
them both together more indissolubly in his service. But
the young engineer's affection was not reciprocated.

He was a light eater, and for years before his death
took little other food than coffee or chocolate, milk, bis-
cuits, raisins and almonds. His dinner usually consisted
of a wheaten roll broken into a bowl of boiled milk. He
never used wine or spirits unless in company. Christopher
Sprenger, a Swede by birth, a member of the Board of
Trade under Pitt, and a warm personal friend of Swedenborg, writing to the Abbe Pernetty, says: "Swedenborg's
knowledge as well as his sincerity was great. He was
constant in friendship, extremely frugal in his diet, and
plain in his dress. His usual food was coffee with milk,

and bread and butter. Sometimes, however, he partook of a little fish, only at rare intervals ate meat, and he never drank above two glasses of wine. He was indifferent to places of honor."

He always lived modestly. For his lodgings in London he paid only at the rate of £14 a year. He kept no servant. When over eighty years of age he was asked if he did not need one. "No," he replied, "an angel is always by my side." It was his habit, after his "illumination," to retire to bed at seven o'clock in the evening, and rise at eight in the morning. One of the simple-minded burgher shopkeepers, with whom he resided in London, was asked if the old gentleman did not require a great deal of attention. "He scarcely requires any," she replied. "The servant has nothing to do for him, except in the morning to lay the fire for him. We trouble ourselves no farther about him. During the day he keeps up the fire himself, and on going to bed takes great care lest the fire should do any damage. He dresses and undresses himself alone, and waits upon himself in everything, so that we scarcely know whether there is anyone in the house or not. I should like him to be with us during the rest of his life. My children will miss him most, for he never goes out without bringing them home some sweets; the little rogues dote upon the old gentleman so much that they prefer him to their own parents."

In the street, Swedenborg usually wore a suit of black velvet, a pair of long ruffles, a curious hilted sword, after the fashion of the times, and a gold-headed cane. He usually spoke very deliberately and distinctly, but stammered a little if he spoke fast. He had no books during the latter period of his life except Bibles, four of different editions in Hebrew and four Latin Bibles. One of his Hebrew Bibles he gave to the pastor of the Swedish church in London as his burial fee. Like Humboldt, he paid little regard to times or seasons, taking his food and repose when nature asked for them.

"Till very lately," says the Rev. Dr. Thomas Hartley, "he (Swedenborg) has not set his name to any of his theological works. He has nothing of the precisian in his manner, nothing of melancholy in his temper, and nothing in the least bordering upon the enthusiast in his conversation or writings,—in the latter of which he delivers facts in the plain style of narrative, speaks of his converse with spirits and angels with the same coolness that he treats of earthly things, as being alike common to him. He proves all points of doctrine from Scripture testimony, always connects charity and good life with true faith, and is upon the whole as rational a divine as I have ever read."[1]

Swedenborg's vision does not seem to have been subject to ordinary limitations. The cases in which he saw what was occurring in different places and beyond the ordinary range of human vision are too well authenticated to be questioned. He was aware of the time when his life on earth would terminate long before his bodily health gave any such premonition. John Wesley, the eminent Methodist, received from Swedenborg the following letter in the latter part of February, 1772:

GREAT BATH STREET, COLDBATH FIELDS, Feb., 1772.

Sir:—I have been informed in the world of spirits that you have a strong desire to converse with me. I shall be happy to see you, if you will favor me with a visit.

I am your humble servant,

EMAN. SWEDENBORG.

Mr. Wesley frankly acknowledged to the company present,—consisting mostly of preachers with whom he was preparing for a circuit, upon which he was about to set out,—that he had been strongly impressed with a desire to see and converse with Swedenborg, and that he had never mentioned that desire to any one. He wrote for answer that he was then closely occupied in preparing for a six months journey, but would do himself the pleasure of waiting upon Swedenborg soon after his return to London. Swedenborg replied that the proposed visit would be too late, as he should himself go into the world of spirits on the 29th day of the next month, never more to return.

---

[1] Dr. Hartley was a clergyman of the church of England, Rector of Winwick in Northamptonshire, a personal acquaintance of Swedenborg, and one of the first receivers of his doctrines.

Mr. Wesley went the circuit, and on his return to London in October learned that Swedenborg had departed this life on the 29th of March preceding.

In the month of December previous he had had an attack of apoplexy, from which he did not recover. He was repeatedly visited during his last illness by Ferelius, the pastor of the Swedish Church in London, who asked him on one occasion if he thought himself about to die, and was answered in the affirmative. It was proposed to him to take the sacrament, and with his assent Ferelius was sent for to administer it. "On this occasion," writes Ferelius, "I remarked to him that, as many persons thought he had only sought fame by his new theological system (which he had attained), he would do well now to publish the truth to the world, and to recant all or any part of what he had erroneously advanced, as he had nothing more to expect from the world, which he was soon to quit forever.

"Upon hearing these words, Swedenborg raised himself half upright in bed, and placing his sound hand on his breast (one was palsied), said with great zeal and emphasis, 'As true as you see me before you, so true is every thing I have written. I could have said more had I been permitted. When you come into eternity you will see all things as I have described them, and we shall have much to say to one another concerning them.'"

When asked if he was disposed to partake of the Holy Supper, he replied:

"Thank you; you mean well, but I do not need it. However, to show the connection between the Church in Heaven and the Church on Earth, I will gladly take it."

Before administering the sacrament, Ferelius asked him if he confessed himself to be a sinner. "Certainly," he answered, "so long as I carry about with me this sinful body." Ferelius continues, "With deep and affecting devotion, and with folded hands, he confessed his unworthiness, and received the Holy Supper. After which he presented me with a copy of his great work, the *Arcana Cœlestia.*"

He told the Shearsmiths, with whom he lived, the day he should die; and their servant said, "he was as pleased as I should have been if I was to have a holiday, or was going to some merry-making."

His faculties were in undiminished vigor to the last. On Sunday afternoon of the 29th day of March, 1772, hearing the clock strike he asked his landlady and her maid, who were both sitting at his bedside, what o'clock it was; and upon being answered it was five o'clock, he said, "It is well; I thank you; God bless you;" and a little after he quietly departed. He had attained the goodly age of eighty-four years.

In the Royal Library of Brussels are four MS. volumes, entitled *Joh. Christian Cuno's Eigenhandige Lebensbeschreibung* (John Christian Cuno's Autobiography), many pages of which are devoted to an account of his acquaintance and intercourse with Swedenborg. Cuno was a great soldier, a merchant, a poet, and a prolific writer. He never embraced the doctrines of Swedenborg,—which lends, perhaps, additional value to the following brief account of his last interview with the Swedish philosopher.

"I shall never forget, as long as I live, the interest he took in me at my own house. It seemed to me as if the truly venerable old man was much more eloquent this last time, and spoke differently from what I had ever heard him speak before. He admonished me to continue in goodness, and to acknowledge the Lord for my God. "If it please God I shall once more come to you in Amsterdam, for I love you."[1] 'O my worthy M. Swedenborg,' I interrupted him, 'that will probably not take place in this world, for I, at least, do not attribute to myself a long life.' 'This you cannot know,' he continued; 'we are obliged to remain in the world as long as the Divine Providence and wisdom see fit. If any one is conjoined with the Lord he has a foretaste of the eternal life in this world; and if he has this he no longer cares so much about this transitory life. Believe me, if I knew that the Lord would call me to Himself to-morrow, I would summon the musicians to-day, in order to be once more really gay in this world.' In order to feel what I then felt you

---

[1] In a marginal note Cuno added, "He was true to his word, for I have conversed with him on 'Change here, Sept. 10, 1770."

would have had to hear the old man say this, in his second childhood. This time, also, he looked so innocent and joyful out of his eyes as I had never seen him look before. I did not interrupt him, and was, as it were, dumb with astonishment. He then saw a Bible lying on my desk, and while I was thus gazing quietly before me, and he could easily see the state of my mind, he took the book and opened it at this passage: 1 John v. 20, 21. 'Read these words,' he said, and then closed the book again. 'But that you may not forget them I will rather put them down for you; and saying this, he dipped the pen into the ink, in order to write them on the leaf, which is preserved here. His hand trembled, however, as may be seen from the figure 1; and this I could not bear. I therefore asked him in a friendly manner to mention the passage to me. I then put down the passage myself. As soon as I had done so, he rose. 'The time now approaches,' he said, 'when I must take leave of my other friends.' He then embraced and kissed me most heartily.

"As soon as he left, I read the passage which he had recommended to me, as follows:—'And we know that the Son of God is come, and hath given us an understanding, that we may know Him that is true; and we are in Him that is true, even in his Son, Jesus Christ. This is the true God, and eternal life. Little children, keep yourselves from idols.'"

On the whole, the most satisfactory contemporaneous opinion of Swedenborg is to be found in a letter addressed to Gen. Tuxen, Inspector-general of Customs at Elsinore, by Count A. J. Von Höpken, who was for many years Prime Minister of Sweden, and one of the most eminent statesmen and writers that country has produced. He has a special claim to the gratitude of mankind, for his active part, in connection with the great naturalist, Linnæus,—who, by the way, was related by marriage to Swedenborg,—in founding the Swedish Academy of Sciences, of which he was the first Secretary. In reply to some inquiries about Swedenborg, with whom he had long been associated in the government, in a letter dated May 11, 1772, Höpken gives the impressions which Swedenborg had left upon his mind during their long official and

friendly intercourse. I cannot better conclude this sketch
of one of the most remarkable of men, than with a few
extracts from these impressions.

. "The office with which I was invested in my country
has often made it my duty to give my opinion in difficult
and delicate matters; but I do not recollect any so delicate ever before to have been submitted to my judgment
as that which you have pleased to propose to me. Senti-
ments and persuasions which one person may entertain
do not always suit others; and what may appear to me
probable, manifest, certain, and incontestible, may to
others seem dark, incomprehensible, and even absurd.
Partly natural organization, partly education, partly pro-
fessional studies, partly prejudices, partly fear of aban-
doning received opinions, and other causes, occasion a
difference of views among men. To unite and settle them
in temporal concerns is not hazardous; but in spiritual
matters, when a tender conscience is to be satisfied, I
have not the spirit requisite for this, and I am also bound
to confess my want of knowledge. All I could say by
way of preliminary on this subject regards the person of
the late Assessor Swedenborg. I have not only known
him these two and forty years, but also, some time since,
daily frequented his company. Though a man who has
lived long in the world, and in my varied career of life
have had numerous opportunities of knowing men, as to
their virtues and vices, their weakness or strength, I do
not remember to have known any man of more uniformly
virtuous character than Swedenborg. Always contented,
never fretful or morose, throughout his life his mind was
occupied with sublime thoughts and speculations. He was
a true philosopher, and lived like one; he labored dili-
gently, and lived frugally without sordidness, he travelled
continually, and his travels cost him no more than if he
had lived at home. He was gifted with a most happy
genius, and a fitness for every science, which made him
shine in all those which he embraced. He was without
contradiction the most learned man in my country; in his
youth he was a great poet. I have in my possession some
remnants of his Latin poetry, which Ovid would not have
been ashamed to own, In his middle age his Latin was

in an easy, elegant and ornamental style; in his later years it was equally clear, but less elegant after he had turned his thoughts to spiritual subjects. He was well acquainted with the Hebrew and Greek; an able and profound mathematician; a happy mechanician,—of which he gave proof in Norway, where, by an easy and simple method he transported the largest galleys over high mountains and rocks, to a gulf where the Danish fleet was stationed. He was likewise a natural philosopher, but on Cartesian principles. He detested metaphysics, as founded on fallacious ideas; because they transcend our sphere, by means of which theology has been drawn from its simplicity and become artificial and corrupted. Having for a long time been Assessor in the College of Mines, he was perfectly conversant with mineralogy; on which science, both as to theory and practice, he also published a valuable and classical work, printed in Leipsic in 1734. If he had remained in his office, his merits and talents would have entitled him to the highest dignity; but he preferred ease of mind, and sought happiness in study.

"In Holland he began to apply himself to anatomy, in which he made singular discoveries, which are preserved somewhere in the *Acta Literaria*. I imagine this science, and his meditations on the effects of the soul upon our curiously constructed body, did by degrees lead him from the material to the spiritual. He possessed a sound judgment upon all occasions; saw everything distinctly, and expressed himself well upon every subject. The most solid memorials, and the best penned, at the Diet of 1761, on matters of finance, were presented by him."

It is worth noting here that the memorials which received these encomiums from the Swedish Prime Minister were presented to the Diet of which Swedenborg was so conspicious and useful a member, at the time when he was in the midst of his spiritual labors. His most voluminous and probably most important theological works, the *Arcana Cælestia* and the *Apocalypse Explained*, besides several smaller works, making together some fifteen quarto volumes, had already been written several years. Their preparation certainly had not prevented his continuing to receive, from his colleagues and contemporaries, the homage which is due, and due only, to a sound understanding and eminent capacity.

In a subsequent letter to the same person Count von Höpken says farther :—

" The late Swedenborg was a pattern of sincerity, virtue and piety, and at the same time, in my opinion, the most learned man in this kingdom ; but all these qualities, which are so many evidences of an honest, virtuous, and pious life, do not at the same time prove that he could not err like other men. What to my judgment may appear evident, convincing and indisputable, may to others appear obscure, complicated and problematical,—so different are our intellectual faculties as well as our education and circumstances ; and hence proceed all the diversities of opinion prevailing among men, which are never to be reconciled. I agree with you, sir, in this, that the Swedenborgian system is more comprehensible by our reason and less complicated than other systems ; and while it forms virtuous men and citizens, it prevents at the same time all kinds of enthusiasm and superstition,—both of which occasion so many and such cruel vexations or ridiculous singularities in the world. And from the present state of religion, more or less everywhere conspicuous according to the more or less free form of government, I am perfectly convinced that the interpolations which men have profusely inserted into religion have nearly effected a total corruption or revolution ; and when this is seen, the Swedenborgian system will become more general, more agreeable, and more intelligible than at present."

No judgment of Swedenborg as a teacher of spiritual truths will deserve to be final or conclusive, that does not take proper notice of one feature of his illuminated writings, which has never failed, we believe, to impress every one who has given them careful consideration. They embrace some thirty octavo volumes ; they deal almost exclusively with spiritual topics and with abstract ideas ; they are not indebted to any pre-existing literature, save the Bible, nor to any science or other repository of accumulated human learning, for a single page of their contents ; they unfold and give minute details of realms into which no human imagination has, so far as we know, within historic times, ever ventured; they offer, at every turn, tests by which, if conflicting with the teachings of the Bible, they could have been at once exposed and consigned to oblivion. And yet we are not aware that any student of Swedenborg has ever succeeded in finding any such conflict, or arriving nearer such a result than a difficulty, and sometimes inability, to comprehend him. In the *Arcana Cœlestia*, in the *Apocalypse Revealed*, and in the *Apocalypse Explained*, we find the interior or correspondential meaning of every word in Genesis, in Exodus, and in the Apocalypse. Many if not most of these words reappear in every other book of the Sacred Scriptures,—where, if they failed to harmonize with the context, they would prove Swedenborg's alleged intercourse with the Lord and His angels a delusion and a fraud, and his doctrine of Correspondences an imposition. If the interior meaning ascribed to a river, or to a mountain, or to a star, or to horses and chariots, to bread, and honey, and the hundreds of other natural objects and phenomena mentioned in the Pentateuch, did not harmonize with the use of these words whenever they occur in the Prophets or in the Evangelists, the discovery would put an end to the study of Swedenborg's spiritual writings as completely as the discovery to-day that the New Testament was forged by some monks in the fourth century would put an end to the use of that portion of the Word in our churches.

Insane people, and even enthusiasts, may reason as acutely and as logically as the soundest thinkers; but in such case, one of their premises at least is always wrong. If it were not, they would not deserve to be called insane or enthusiasts. There is no difficulty in detecting the point where the weakness of such minds betrays itself. No one, so far as I am aware, has ever convicted Swedenborg of being inconsistent with himself in any construction he has ever put upon any sentence or word of the Sacred Scriptures, nor in anything he has communicated of the states of existence beyond the grave. Whatever else may be said of his teachings, they are certainly not the incoherent combinations of an unsound mind.

Cuno, from whose memoirs I have already quoted, who

had some smattering of Swedenborg's philosophy, but no sympathy with his distinctive doctrines, complained of the theologians of his day for not exposing Swedenborg's "heresies." "This new teacher," he says, "who has no authority to show for his mission, denies most deliberately before the whole world, the resurrection of the flesh, . . and the whole world keeps silence. Methinks it is by no means sufficient to look upon the good and honest Swedenborg simply in the light of a madman, and meanwhile give him permission to write and print what he pleases.

"If there was an ignorant man whose impudence was proportioned to his ignorance, it was the notorious John Ch. Edelman, who has now been dead for many years. This man,—who was in comparison with the profoundly learned and pious Swedenborg, a beastly blasphemer of the Word of God and of the Church,—raised against himself whole armies of scholars, by whom he was refuted. A silly fellow like him was not worth such treatment. I am by no means able to contend with the honest Swedenborg; yet, if eleven years ago a thorough theologian had taken up his *Heaven and Hell*, if he had acknowledged all the good it contained and quietly refuted its errors, he had thereby made him more cautious about flooding the world with his writings, if he did not cure him of his vagaries."

Speaking again of *The New Jerusalem and its Heavenly Doctrine*, which had just been published, he recurred to this subject, "It may in truth be said of it, 'good and evil things are here mixed together.' I at least am willing, nay constrained, to confess that he has said many things of which I never thought.

"No scholar, versed in science himself, will question Swedenborg's science. It does not seem to me sufficient for a theologian, who from pride or indolence is unwilling to examine his works, to shout with Festus, 'Swedenborg is beside himself; much learning hath made him mad;' or for others who would be considered faithful watchmen on the walls of Zion to say superciliously, 'The good that Swedenborg has said is old, and the new worthless.' I admit there may be some truth in this; still, if the theologians whose vocation it is to examine and defend the truth had acted conscientiously, they would not have kept so long silent, nor allowed this man to write unchallenged all these things, which may or may not be true. I have listened to the judgment of many men concerning Swedenborg. Some, especially such as know the character of this man, have pitied him; others have called him visionary. A certain young scholar who had only read his *De Amore Conjugiale* was inclined to consider him a Socinian. I could very easily convince him that he had but turned over the leaves of his book, or had read without reflection. If ever there has been a zealous Anti-Arian and Anti-Socinian that man without doubt was Emanuel Swedenborg."

Cuno's persistent and sensible appeal, now after the lapse of a century, is as seasonable and as sensible as it ever was. No one has yet proved equal to the task to which Cuno invited the theologians of his day, nor been able to convict the oracle of the New Church in any instance of inconsistency with himself. We are not aware that the difficulty of such a task has diminished with the lapse of time.

As an ethical writer, Swedenborg has no peer in any literature outside of the Bible. No other man has so clearly defined the boundaries which divide the right from the wrong in the human conduct, nor made the path of duty so consistently plain, nor furnished so many good reasons for walking in it. It is to be regretted that the prejudices which have prevailed against him in the ecclesticial world, but which happily are fast fading out, have prevented his works from receiving from ethical writers the attention they deserve.

It seems hardly credible that a writer so learned and so catholic in his literary tastes and judgments as Sir James Macintosh, should have attempted to write a history of the progress of Ethical Philosophy without once mentioning the name of Swedenborg. It may even be doubted if he ever opened one of Swedenborg's works. It is yet more remarkable that the best treatise on Ethical Science that has been written prior or subsequent to Swedenborg's time, *Christian Ethics*, by Dr. H. Martensen, should not contain an allusion to the teachings of the greatest authority living or dead upon that subject.

A careful perusal of Bishop Martensen's masterly work jus-
tifies the belief that he was no stranger to, but a diligent
student rather, of Swedenborg's writings ; but like many
others occupying high station in the Church, he may have
doubted whether his recognition of Swedenborg as one
of his guides would not have impaired his authority with
the class of readers he was addressing. Coleridge had the
courage to say that "as a moralist, Swedenborg is above
all praise. And it is safe to predict that any book which
shall fairly embody the ethical teachings of Swedenborg,
would soon displace every treatise on Ethical Science that
has yet been printed.

The principles by which Swedenborg governed his conduct in life,—as is abundantly confirmed by the whole
course of his singularly disinterested career,—it is interesting to find expressed in a few simple rules, that were
found among his MSS. They show that he tried at least
to exemplify in his life the lessons of which he was the
incomparable teacher. They are as follows :—

1. Often to read and meditate on the Word of God.

2. To submit everything to the will of the Divine
Providence.

3. To observe in everything a propriety of deportment,
and to keep the conscience clear.

4. To discharge with fidelity the functions of my em-
ployments, and the duties of my office, and to make myself in all things useful to society. [1]

---

[1] Bacon's view of an ideal life is expressed in fewer words, and it is interesting to note its points of resemblance to and difference from that of Swedenborg.
"Certainly," says Bacon, "it is heaven upon earth to have a man's mind move
in charity, rest in Providence and turn upon the poles of truth." He omits only
Swedenborg's fourth point, "to make myself in all things useful to society;" but
what an omission, as understood and taught by Swedenborg!

APPENDIX.

LITERARY, SCIENTIFIC, AND PHILOSOPHICAL WORKS.

1. Select Sentences of L. Annæus Seneca and Pub. Syrus Mimus, with the annotations of Erasmus, and the Greek version of Jos. Scaliger, which, with the consent of the Philosophical Society, and furnished with notes, are submitted with diffidence to public examination, by Emanuel Swedberg, Upsal, 1709, 92 pages 8vo.

2. The Swedish poem "The Rule of Youth and the Mirror of Old Age" from Ecclesiastes XII., by Dr. Jasper Swedberg, Bishop of Scara, the best of fathers, translated into Latin verse, by his son, Emanuel Swedberg, Scara, 1709.

3. To Sophia Elisabeth Brenner, the only Muse of our age, when she edited her poems a second time. London, 1710, 2 pages 4to.

4. The Northern Muse sporting with the Deeds of Heroes and Heroines: or Fables similar to those of Ovid, under various names. By Emanuel Swedberg, Greifswalde, 1715, 112 pages 16mo.

5. The Heliconian Sport, or Miscellaneous Poems, written in various places, by Emanuel Swedberg, Scara, 1716, 16 pages 4to.

6. A Sapphic Poem in celebration of August 28, 1716, the birthday of my dearest father, Doctor Jasper Swedberg, the Right Reverend Bishop of Scara, when he was sixty-three years old, which is "the great climacteric year." Scara, 1716.

7. Dædalus Hyperboreus, or some new mathematical and physical experiments and observations, made by the Honorable Assessor Polhem and other ingenious men in Sweden, and which will be made public from time to time for the general good. Upsal, 1716–1718, six numbers, 154 pages 4to.

8. Information concerning the Tinware of Stiensund, its use and the method of tinning. Stockholm, 1717, 4 pages, 4to.

9. The Importance of establishing an Astronomical Observatory in Sweden, with a plan by which this may be carried out. 4 pages MS. large folio, 1717.

10. On the Causes of Things, 4 pages MS. 4to. 1717

11. A new Theory concerning the End of the Earth, MS. fragment of 38 pages, 1717.

12. On a Mode of assisting Commerce and Manufactures, MS. 6 pages, 4to, 1717.

13. A Memorial on the establishment of Saltworks in Sweden. MS. 4 pages folio, 1717.

14. The Nature of Fire and Colors, MS. 6 pages folio, 1717.

15. Algebra, edited in ten books, Upsala, 135 pages, 16mo, 1718.

16. Contributions to Geometry and Algebra. MS. 169 pages, 4to, 1718.

17. An Attempt to find the East and West Longitude by the Moon, set forth for the judgment of the learned. Upsala, 1718, 38 pages 8vo.

18. On the Motion and Repose of the Earth and the Planets, i. e. some arguments showing that the earth slackens its speed more than heretofore, causing winter and summer nights and days to be longer, in respect to time, than formerly. Scara, 1718, 40 pages, 16 mo.

19. Respecting the great Depths of Water, and of strong Tides in the primeval world ; proofs from Sweden. Upsala, 1719, 40 pages, 16mo.

20. A Description of Swedish iron furnaces, and of the processes for smelting iron, 84 pages 4to, 1719.

21. Anatomy of our most subtle Nature, showing that our moving and our living force consists of vibrations. MS. 48 pages, 4to, 1719.

22. New Directions for discovering Metallic Veins, or some hints hitherto unknown for the discovery of mineral veins and treasures deeply hidden in the earth. Ms. 14 pages 4to.

23. Information concerning Docks, Canal-locks, and Saltworks. Stockholm, 1719, 8 pages 4to.

24. Proposal for regulating our Coinage and Measures, by which our computation is facilitated and fractions are abolished. Stockholm, 1719, 8 pages 4to.

25. Concerning the Rise and Fall of Lake Wenner, and how far this is due to the flow of water into it, and the carrying off of water by streams. MS. 7 pages folio, 1720.

26. First Principles of Natural Things, deduced from experience and geometry, or *a posteriori* and *a priori*. MS. 560 pages, 4to, 1720.

27. Letter of Emanuel Swedenborg to Jacob à Melle. In Acta Literaria Sueciæ for 1721, 4 pages (192 to 196).

28. A Forerunner of the First Principles of Natural Things, or of new attempts to explain Chemistry and experimental Physics geometrically. Amsterdam, 1721, 199 pages, 16mo.

29. New Observations and Discoveries respecting Iron, and Fire, and particularly respecting the elementary nature of fire,

together with a new construction of Stoves. Amsterdam, 1721, 56 pages, 16mo. illustrated.

30. A new Method of finding the Longitudes of Places, on land and at sea, by Lunar Observations. Amsterdam, 1721, 29 pages, 8vo.

31. A new Mechanical Plan for constructing Docks and Dykes; and a mode of discovering the powers of Vessels by the application of Mechanical Principles. Amsterdam, 1721, 21 pp. 8vo, (second edition, 1727).

32. New Rules for maintaining Heat in Rooms. In Acta Lit. Sueciæ for 1722, 3 pages.

33. Miscellaneous Observations on the things of Nature, and especially on Minerals, Fire and the Strata of Mountains. Part I. to III. Leipzig, 164 pages, 16mo. Part IV., Schiffbeck near Hamburg, 56 pages 16mo, 1722.

34. Fable of the Love and Metamorphosis of the Muse Urania into a man and servant of Apollo, addressed to the most illustrious and excellent Senator, Count Maurice Wellingk, Schiffbeck near Hamburg, 1722, 8 pages, 4to.

35. An Elucidation of a Law of Hydrostatics, demonstrating the Power of the deepest Waters of the Deluge and their Action on the Rocks and other Substances at the bottom of the Sea. In Acta Lit. Sueciæ for 1722, pp. 353 to 356.

36. Frank Views on the Fall and Rise in the Value of Swedish Money. Stockholm, 1722, 20 pages, 4to.

37. The Magnet and its Qualities. MSS. 299 pp. 4to. 1722.

38. On the right Treatment of Metals. MS. 1723. 1481 pages, 4to.

39. The Motion of the Elements in General. MS. 5 pages, 4to. (1724 to 1733.)

40. Papers belonging to the Principia, etc. MS. 13 pages 4to. (1724 to 1733.)

41. The Mechanism of the Soul and Body. MS. 16 pages 4to. (1724 to 1733.)

42. A Comparison of Christian Wolf's Ontology and Cosmology with Swedenborg's *"Principia Rerum Naturalium."* MS. 49 pages 4to. (1724 to 1733.)

43. Anatomical Observations. MS. 6 pages 4to. (1724 to 1733.)

44. Journal of Travels for the Years 1733 and 1734. MS. 80 pages 4to.

45. Philosophical and Metallurgical Works. By Emanuel Swedenborg, 3 vols., Dresden and Leipzig, 1734. First vol., 452 pp. folio, 2d vol., 386 pages, 3d vol., 534 pages.

46. Outlines of a Philosophical Argument on the Infinite and the Final Cause of Creation, and on the Mechanism of the Operation of Soul and Body. Dresden and Leipzig, 1734, pp. 270, 8vo.

47. An Abstract of the Work entitled *Principia Rerum Naturalium.* MS. 27 pp. 4to. 1734.

48. Fragments of three Treatises on the Brain, MS. 1004 pages 4to, 1734–1738.

49. Description of my Journeys. MS. 40 pages, 4to. 1736 to 1739.

50. The Way to a Knowledge of the Soul. MS. 5 pages 4to. 1738.

51. Faith and Good Works. MS. 10 pp. 4to. 1738.

52. Economy of the Animal Kingdom. London and Amsterdam. Part I., 1740, pp. 388, 4to, Part II., 1741, pp. 194, 4to.

53. A Characteristic and Mathematical Philosophy of Universals. MS. 5 pages folio, 1740.

54. On the Bones of the Skull, and Ossification, and the Dura Mater. MS. 49 p. fol., 1740.

55. A Summary of Corpuscular Philosophy. MS. 1 page, folio, 1740.

56. Anatomy of all the Parts of the Larger and Lesser Brains ; of the *Medulla Oblongata and Spinalis ;* together with the Diseases of the Head. MS. 636 pp. fol., 1740.

57. Introduction to a Rational Psychology, the first part of which treats of the fibre, the arachnoid tunic, and the diseases of the fibres. MS. 366 pp. 4to. 1740 and 1741.

58. On the Declination of the Magnetic Needle ; a Controversy between E. Swedenborg and Prof. A. Celsius of Upsal. Read and discussed before the Academy of Science at Stockholm in 1740 and 1749.

59. Introduction to a Rational Psychology, Part II, treating of the Doctrine of Correspondences and Representations. MS. 9 pages folio. 1741.

60. A Hieroglyphic Key to Natural and Spiritual Mysteries, by way of Representations and Correspondences. MS. 48 pages 4to. 1741.

61. Comparison of the Three Theories concerning the intercourse between the Soul and the Body. MS. 44 pages 4to. 1741.

62. The Red Blood. MS. 24 pages 4to. 1741.

63. The Animal Spirit. MS. 24 pages 4to. 1741.

64. Sensation, or Passion of the Body. MS. 11 pages 4to. 1741.

65. Origin and Propagation of the Soul. MS. 6 pages 4to. 1741.

66. Action. MS. 30 pages 4to. 1741.

67. Rational Psychology. MS. 234 pages folio. 1741 and 1742.

68. Signification of Philosophical Terms, or Ontology. MS. 21 pages folio. 1742.

69. The Anatomy of the Human Body. MS. 269 pages folio.

70. Digest of Swammerdam's Biblia Naturæ. MS. 79 pages folio. 1743.

71. The Animal Kingdom considered Anatomically, Physically and Philosophically. Hague, 1744. Part I., pp. 438. Part II., pp. 286, 4to.

72. Swedenborg's Private Diary for 1743 and 1744. MS. 101 pages, 16mo.

73. On Sense in general, its influx into the Soul, and the reaction of the latter. MS. 200 pages folio. 1744.

74. The Muscles of the Face and Abdomen. MS. pages 13 folio. 1744.

75. Physical and Optical Experiments. MS. pp. 6 folio. 1744.

76. On the Brain. MS. 43 pages folio. 1744.

77. The Animal Kingdom, considered Anatomically, etc. Part III, 169 pages 4to. London, 1745.

THEOLOGICAL WORKS.

1. The Worship and Love of God. London, 1745. Part I. pp. 120, 4to. Part II. pp. 24, 4to.

2. The Worship and Love of God. Part III. 9 pp. 4to, printed in proof-sheets and in MS., 1745.

3. The History of Creation as related by Moses. MS. 25 pp. 1745.

4. The Messiah about to come into the World, and the Kingdom of God. MS. pp. 32, 1745.

5. Explanation of the Historical Word of the Old Testament. MS. 3 vol, pp. 169 fol. 1745–6.

6. Biblical Index to the Historical Books of the Old Testament. MS. pp. 581, 1746.

7. Explanation of Isaiah and Jeremiah. MS. 107 pp, folio, 1746–7.

8. Notes on Jeremiah and the Book of Lamentations. MS. on the margin of his Latin Bible. 1746–7.

9. Biblical Index to Isaiah and a portion of Jeremiah and Genesis. MS. 1746–7.

10. Memorabilia, Part I. MS. 1747.

11. Fragments of Notes on Genesis and Exodus. MS. 1747.

12. Fragments of Notes on the Prophets. MS. 1747.

13. Names of Men, Countries, Kingdoms and Towns in the Sacred Scriptures. MS. 245 pp. folio. 1746–8.

14. Biblical Index to the Prophetical Books of the Old Testament, the Psalms, Job, the Apocalypse ; and likewise to Exodus, Leviticus, Numbers, and Deuteronomy. MS. 636 pp. folio large. 1747–8.

15. Biblical Index of the New Testament. MS. pp. 435, large oblong folio. 1747–8.

16. Memorabilia, Part II. MS. 516 pp. oblong folio. 1747–8.

17. The Heavenly Mysteries which are in the Sacred Scrip-

tures or the Word of the Lord disclosed ; here, those which are in *Genesis*, together with Wonderful Things which have been seen in the World of Spirits, and in the Heaven of Angels. London, 1747 to 1753, 5 vols. 2761 pp. 4to.

18. The Heavenly Mysteries, etc. ; here those which are in *Exodus*, together with, etc. 3 vols, 1796 pp. 4to. London. 1747–58.

19. Memorabilia, Part III. MS. 1748–50. In the printed copy it fills 372 pages 8vo.

20. Memorabilia Part IV. MS. 134 pp. 16mo. 1750–51.

21. Index to the Adversaria and the Memorabilia, Part I. to IV. MS. 988 pp. folio. 1748–51.

22. Memorabilia, Part V. MS. 602 pages 8vo. 1752 to 1765.

23. Index to the Memorabilia, Part III–IV. MS. 100 pp. folio. 1752–65.

24. Index to the Words, Names and Things in the *Arcana Cœlestia*. MS. 1749 to 1756.

25. Heaven and its Wonders and Hell ; from Things heard and seen. London, 1758, 272 pp. 4to.

26. The White Horse mentioned in Revelations XIX ; and afterwards, the Word and its spiritual or internal Sense from the *Arcana Cœlestia*. London, 1748, 23 pp. 4to.

27. The New Jerusalem and its Heavenly Doctrine ; from things heard out of Heaven ; with an Introduction on the New Heaven, and the New Earth. London, 1758, 155 pp. 4to.

28. The Earths in our Solar System, which are called Planets, and the Earths in the Starry Heavens ; their Inhabitants, and also the Spirits and Angels from there ; from Things heard and seen. London, 1758, 72 pp. 4to.

29. The Last Judgment, and the Destruction of Babylon, showing that what was foreteld in the Book of Revelation has been fulfilled at the present day ; from Things heard and seen. London, 1758, 55 pp. 4to.

30. The Apocalypse explained according to its spiritual sense, wherein are revealed the Mysteries therein foretold, which have hitherto been unknown. MS. 1992 pp. 4 vols, 4to.

31. On the Athanasian Creed. MS. 42 pp. 8vo. 1759.

32. The Lord. MS. 42 pp. 8vo. 1759.

33. A Summary Exposition of the internal sense of the Prophetical Books and the Psalms of the Old Testament ; to which are added some things respecting the Historical parts of the Word. MS. oblong folio, 125 pp. 8vo. 1759–60.

33a. Papers prepared for the Swedish Diet. MS. 100 pages folio. 1760.

34. The Last Judgment. MS. 160 pp. oblong folio. 1760.

35. The Spiritual World. MS. 30 pp. oblong folio. 1760.

36. The Sacred Scriptures or Word of the Lord, from experience. MS. 42 pages, 8vo. 1761.

37. On the Precepts of the Decalogue. MS. 6 pp. 8vo. 1761.

38. Observations on Faith. MS. 2 pp. oblong folio. 1761.
39. The Doctrine of the New Jerusalem respecting the Lord. Amsterdam, 1763, 64 pp. 4to.
40. The Doctrine of the New Jerusalem respecting the Sacred Scripture. Amsterdam, 1763, 54 pp. 4to.
41. The Doctrine of Life for the New Jerusalem, from the precepts of the Decalogue. Amsterdam, 1763, 36 pp. 4to.
42. The Doctrine of the New Jerusalem respecting Faith. Amsterdam, 1763, 23 pp. 4to.
43. Continuation of the Treatise on the Last Judgment and the Spiritual World. Amsterdam, 1763, 28 pp. 4to.
44. Description of the Mode in which marble slabs are inlaid for tables and other ornaments. In "Transactions of the Royal Academy of Sciences," April–June, 1763, vol. XXIV. pp. 107–113.
45. The Divine Love. MS. 22 pp. oblong folio. 1762–63.
46. The Divine Wisdom. MS. 46 pp. oblong folio. 1763.
47. Angelic Wisdom respecting the Divine Love and Divine Wisdom. Amsterdam, 1763, 151 pp. 4to.
48. Angelic Wisdom respecting the Divine Providence. Amsterdam, 1764, 214 pp. 4to.
49. Doctrine of Charity. MS. 49 pp. large folio. 1764.
50. The Apocalypse Revealed, wherein are disclosed the Mysteries there foretold, which have hitherto remained concealed. Amsterdam, 1766, 629 pp. 4to.
51. New Method of finding the Longitude of Places on Land and at Sea. Amsterdam, 1766, 8 pp. 4to.
52. On the Horse, and Hieroglyphics. MS. 1766.
53. Index of Words, Names and Things contained in the Apocalypse Revealed. MS. 75 pp. 4to. 1766.
54. Five Memorabilia. MS. 13 pp. folio. 1766.
55. Conversation with Angels. MS. 3 pp. folio. 1766.
56. First work on Conjugial Love. MS. 1766–7.
57. Memorabilia on Marriage. MS. 13 pp. large folio. 1766.
58. The Wise Delights of Conjugial Love ; after which follow the Insane Pleasures of Scortatory Love. Amsterdam, 1768, pp. 328, 4to.
59. The Natural and Spiritual Sense of the Word. MS. 1768.
60. Justification and Good Works : Conversations with Calvin, etc. MS. 1768.
61. Outlines of the Doctrine of the New Church. MS. 1768.
62. A brief Exposition of the Doctrine of the New Church which is meant by the New Jerusalem in the Apocalypse. Amsterdam, 1769, 4to.
63. The Intercourse between the Soul and the Body, which is supposed to take place either by physical influx or by spiritual influx or by preëstablished harmony. London, 1769.
64. Answer to a Letter written by a Friend. London, 1769, 3 pp. 4to.

65. Nine Questions concerning the Trinity, etc., proposed by Thomas Hartley to Emanuel Swedenborg ; with his Answers. MS. pp. 6, 4to. 1769.

66. The Canons or entire Theology of the New Church. MS. pp. 45, folio. 1769.

67. Corroborating Passages from the Old and New Testaments, collected and briefly explained. MS. pp. 39, folio. 1769.

68. The True Christian Religion, containing the Universal Theology of the New Church which was predicted by the Lord in Daniel VII. 13–14, and in the Apocalypse XXI, 1, 2 ; by Emanuel Swedenborg, Servant of the Lord Jesus Christ. Amsterdam, 1771, pp. 541, 4to.

69. Materials for the True Christian Religion. MS. pp. 23 folio. 1770.

70. Ecclesiastical History of the New Church. MS. 1 p. folio. 1771.

71. A Summary of the Coronis or Appendix to the True Christian Religion ; containing an Account of the four Churches on this Earth since the Creation of the World, and of their periods and consummations. Likewise an account of the New Church about to succeed these Four, which will be a truly Christian Church. MS. 1771.

72. The Consummation of the Age, the Lord's Second Coming, and the New Church ; to which is added an Invitation to that Church addressed to the whole Christian World. MS. pp. 15 folio. 1771.